# WEB OF DARKNESS

## LA DARK SERIES
## BOOK 2

# PARIS ANDREN

J JAF Publishing, LLC
Kansas City, MO

*In Memory of my Andrea*

And within her point of darkness—she found home.

—AVA DELANEY

# Hotel Dark

Once you checked in to Hotel Dark, you never checked out.

An appropriate slogan for the roach motel where they were kept. It reminded her of those commercials from long ago. Except to check in to Hotel Dark you were drugged, kidnapped, and forced to sell your body to whomever wanted to purchase it—be it for the hour, the night, or indefinitely—until they eventually sold you on the black market.

You had no choices.

There was no discriminating.

Whoever paid for you, was allowed to have you.

There was no time off or time out—ever.

The money for selling your body went to your handlers. Your body belonged to them. So the dirty cash lined their pockets and not your own. It was modern day slavery at its worst.

And it was hiding in plain sight.

She was just one of the many lost and forgotten. Nothing special, after all, and pathetically naive.

But not naive anymore—they had stripped the innocence from her on that first day, along with her clothes and her pride. She'd been left with nothing except her regrets and her memories.

She'd left the suffocation of her parents' home to pursue the career she knew she was meant to have. She would be an actress on the big screen.

She ignored all the naysayers who told her how hard it was to be discovered in Hollywood. They were just jealous.

She had something all those other deluded people didn't have—a natural affinity for acting. Didn't she have her high school's coveted Tony for best actress to prove it? It also helped that she was naturally pretty. She had a Jennifer Aniston haircut and color and big green eyes. She tended to be on the thin side, but she worked out every day to keep toned.

So she had set off for Hollywood with that golden Tony packed in to her bag, the cash that she had stolen from her parents' *mad money* jar, and a pocket full of hope.

She had a plan. She had life goals to attain. She would be a big star—on the big screen!

She'd prove them all wrong. It was time she took control of her own life. She was an adult now.

Now, if she could find the rewind button, she'd pound on that bitch until it broke and she was home again—happily suffocating. But sadly, there were no do overs.

So here she was—consigned to hell and barely surviving this dark world.

She had no idea how long she'd been there, as the days and the months had blurred into one long, endless moment of unending degradation.

Occasionally she was drugged and could momentarily forget the fucked-up reality that was now her life. But more often than not, she was painfully lucid and begging for the drugs' blessed euphoria.

It was a love-hate relationship with the drugs. She loved the escape but hated the loss of control; hated how they made her act; hated what they made her do.

But mostly she hated herself and what she had become. The guards' little whore. *Blayd* they called her—*whore* in Russian.

She would do whatever it took to survive. Whatever it took to *not* be shipped off to the black market. She knew that was the key to seeing her parents again. To seeing her little sister, who looked up to her as a role model.

She was no one's role model now. Far from it.

The guards visited her every day or so it seemed. She had no contact with anyone at Hotel Dark, except the men that came and went on a daily basis, but they didn't count. All the inmates, she thought of them as such, were locked in their own rooms. They had no contact with one another.

She was imprisoned in room 209.

She knew that much, as the room number was printed on the phone that sat on the nightstand.

She tried to use it on that first day, but it had been hopelessly dead and had remained so. Despite that, she continued to pick up that damned receiver every day to check it—just in case.

More than once she had thought about destroying the phone, just to keep it from mocking her. She had even gone so far as to unplug it, once or twice, but that was as brave as she had ever managed to be.

It was Thursday night the guard told her when she'd asked at the end of his *visit*. It was too hard to keep track. Especially when minimal light filtered into her room and one day blended into the next. Difficult to differentiate between night and day—was it the sun or street lights between the cracks? Who knew?

She should have kept better track of the days. But she had been too scared and too drugged in the beginning to think of it. Now that she had, there was nothing to write with—not a pen, not a pencil—nothing.

Not until she had stepped on a loose carpet tack one hundred and eighty hash-marks ago. That was when she had started scoring the drywall in the closet. She'd felt brilliant and innovative for thinking of it—until she'd opened the closet door.

The walls had already been scored with two hundred and thirty-five hash-marks on one side and one hundred and twenty on the other. She ignored both walls and their implications. She chose a bare portion of the closet wall to start her own rows. The flaking beige paint stuck irritatingly to the bottom of her dirty feet. She ignored that too.

She had a goal.

She would leave this place before she surpassed the number of hash-marks gouged into the closet wall. The ones on the right side that is.

That was her plan. It was a good plan. Not well thought out, but she decided she'd improvise when the time came.

Every moment that she wasn't on her back in that disgusting bed, she sat by the door and listened. The stupid guards would chatter amongst themselves before visiting her room. Usually they came in one at a time—but not always.

All her vigilant listening had finally paid off. She heard the guards mention that they would be cleaning house.

Tomorrow.

A bad feeling settled in the pit of her stomach. She knew they weren't talking about breaking out the vacuum and some lemon Pledge.

She would have to achieve her goal tomorrow—one way or another—she was leaving.

# CHAPTER ONE

# Ava

Startled awake, I sat up with a gasp.

"I'm sorry, Ava. I didn't mean to stop so quickly," apologized my fiancé, Detective Sage Cartier.

Embarrassed, first I fidgeted with my clothes and then with the tail-end of my braided hair—that was coiled in my lap. "It's not your fault, Sage. I was pretty out of it."

I'd been trapped in another nightmare. Drifting somewhere between asleep and awake. In a twilight of sorts. So when we had pulled into the driveway of the cabin and stopped—I was abruptly pulled from the dreamscape within my mind.

I welcomed the interruption and the wakefulness—as my nightmares continued to remain veiled in darkness. Their shadowy illusiveness caused my heart to race and my body to ache with remembered pain.

I didn't mention the frequency of my nightmares to Sage—there was no reason to. Besides, I didn't want to add to his worries. I told myself I would share when the right opportunity presented itself.

A couple months ago, I reached out to my physician about the nightmares. Dr. Wong had treated me post-rape and post-abduction a few months ago. I felt close to her, despite the unusual circumstances surrounding our introduction.

Dr. Wong had explained that the frequency and the intensity of these nightmares might actually be new memories trying to surface. That my subconscious mind could try to piece together seemingly random events to create a clearer picture of what had occurred when I'd been abducted.

She felt that these dreams were a part of my emotional recovery. *Dreaming* to understand.

But they weren't dreams—they were nightmares.

Plain and simple.

I just couldn't remember them and honestly I didn't want to.

Marcus Oliver had been a fellow dancer and a friend—or so I had thought. He'd organized and instigated my abduction with the help of his ex-girlfriend, ballerina Natalia Vinokourov—my cousin. Though I didn't realize that little tidbit until much later.

I met Marcus and Natalia earlier this year at Madame's dance studio. A renowned Prima Ballerina herself, Madame offered an exclusive ballet intensive to help dancers prepare for the open auditions at the LA Ballet, as well as for other local dance companies.

Madame had taken me under her wing for private instruction. It had been quite the surprising coup and I had been ecstatic about the honor. Madame had asked Marcus to help us with the partnering portion of her lessons. He was a phenomenal dancer, beautifully muscled like most dancers—tall and handsome with blonde hair and dark brown eyes that were almost black.

He would have been a wonderful partner for the pas de deux portion of the tryouts—except that he had started to creep me out. It was the way he looked at me and touched me, beyond what what was needed for our partnering. I should have known something wasn't right —but I'd been so naive and far too trusting. I wish I would have known what had been hiding behind those good looks and black eyes.

At the end of the intensive, we were lucky enough to perform our practice solo routines at the Shrine Auditorium. Dancing across that historic stage had been an incredible moment for me.

I treasured that magical memory of *before*.

Before I'd been deceived. Before I'd been betrayed. Before I'd been drugged and kidnapped.

Before I had been forced to transform into this new Ava.

I was accustomed to her now—this new Ava—but I still ached for what had been and would never be.

Marcus and his sadistic boss, Ivan Dubrovsky, were both sociopathic rapists and were involved in human trafficking. Unfortunately, I had caught their unwanted attention and paid the price for doing so—through no fault of my own.

But Marcus was dead now, presumably killed by Ivan. And Sage and I had fled LA to escape Ivan's obsession with me. It wasn't enough for him to have kidnapped me twice and to have raped me—no he wanted to destroy me and Sage as well.

We had disrupted his dark world.

I peeked quickly at Sage, then away. Concern was etched on his face. I turned away before he could see through the transparency of mine.

"Where are we?" I asked, my voice husky from grief and from sleeping the past few hours. I knew that we must be in the mountains somewhere north of LA. But I couldn't see the landscape, as dawn had yet to breach the dark of night.

"Hours from LA, but in a place where I know we'll be safe."

"Safe sounds heavenly, especially with how life has been lately."

"I know, Beauty," he said, "Keeping you safe is my first priority. The cabin and its property are nestled on a secluded stretch of land. No one in LA knows of their existence."

I loved that Sage still called me Beauty. He had done so from almost the moment I had passed out in his arms when we first met at L'Inked Tattoo Studio. His friend, Carter James had been shocked to find Sage sitting on the floor and cradling me in his arms. He had asked Sage where *Sleeping Beauty* had come from and according to Sage, the name had perfectly suited me, though I had been quite the *abused* Sleeping Beauty at the time.

Sage picked up my left hand and rubbed his thumb across my engagement ring, as he had done so numerous times throughout the night. I felt loved and incredibly safe in his capable hands.

I loved being his. My ring was a sign of his commitment and ownership. Not a trendy sentiment these days. But I didn't care.

I loved the idea of being owned by him. And owning him in return.

I turned my hand over and gripped his tight, acknowledging his thoughtfulness. His protective nature.

"When we wake up in the morning, I'll show you around. It's very tranquil here. You'll see," Sage said, contemplative.

"It's a place where I've come to escape the grind of life. My grandfather Pete willed this mountain cabin to me, along with the Laurel Canyon home—five years ago when he died," Sage said, a note of sadness coloring his voice.

"I can't wait to see everything. Do you think we'll be here for long?" I asked.

"I don't know. I'm hoping that Trey and the Lieut. will be able to solve the mystery of where that rat-bastard Ivan is hiding. And sooner rather than later."

Sage turned the headlights on so that we could see to walk into the cabin. But when I would have joined him, he asked me to wait. He wanted to open the door, turn on the lights, and walk through the cabin first. I flushed with warmth at his thoughtful gesture.

He told me that the cabin should be ready for us. His caretakers came once a month to clean and freshen-up the inside. We had stopped outside of town to buy a week's worth of groceries.

Lordy, I was tired. I couldn't wait to lay down and have a proper sleep. Sage had to be exhausted too. He had driven the entire time and was still recovering from his injuries.

"Everything's safe," Sage said, when he returned to the car.

I was leaning against his restored 1965 cherry-red Mustang when Sage returned. He walked straight to me and pulled me into his arms. Home, he felt like home to me.

He kissed my lips with a gentle brushing of his and said, "Let's get ready for bed. We both need some sleep."

"Lead the way. I'm more than ready, despite the fact that I slept most of the way here," I smiled up at him.

By the look Sage gave me, he saw through my attempts at levity.

Hard to sleep when nightmares are running through your mind and you're left chasing ghosts.

While I washed up, Sage brought our belongings in and locked all the doors. He started a fire in the bedroom fireplace. It was cold out and the temperature would drop down into the forties before morning.

Crawling into the beautifully carved sleigh bed to wait for Sage, I moved over to the far side. I knew Sage would want to lay between me and the door. He was always protecting me.

"Come in here and warm me up," I beckoned, as he came towards the bed.

He slid between the sheets and pulled me into the cradle of his hips. Close to his naked skin.

"I'll hold you close to my heart, Beauty—the whole night through and every night thereafter." He placed light kisses along my neck and shoulders. "I missed you so much while I was away and recovering. Those were dark days, Ava—for both of us."

Sage and my father, Alexei Vinokourov, had found the warehouse where Ivan had been keeping me.

Drugged and bound, I had been useless in my own escape. They had stormed the building to rescue me, but Sage had paid a heavy price for his attempt. He had nearly died when Ivan had shot him multiple times in the chest.

He had endured months of agonizing rehabilitation and I had endured those months—alone—thinking he was dead—before he had recovered enough to return to me. He surprised me at The Grand Auditorium the night of my first solo performance as a principal dancer for the Los Angeles Ballet.

They hosted a special engagement that night featuring concert pianist, Riley Spencer. I had been chosen as the soloist to dance to her accompaniment. She and I had since become close friends.

The night was bittersweet. I was celebrating, as my dreams were finally coming true, yet I was sad too. It was such an emotional piece that I performed that night. But it suited my new, darker style of dancing. I remember feeling as if my soul were raw and bleeding all over that beautiful stage.

At the end of the finale, I found myself surrounded by a beautiful carpet of roses and to my complete amazement, I received a standing ovation. And in typical Ava fashion, I curtsied and just about fell over due to my shaky legs. I'd been emotional and not very graceful I thought.

One of the ushers had brought over a bouquet of exquisite, long stemmed roses in a blushed pink. They were so beautiful...

*My mind was still so caught up in the performance and intoxicated by the heady fragrance of the roses, that I wasn't paying attention to where I was going once I was off stage.*

*Reluctantly, I pulled my face from the flowers and stopped abruptly. I dropped the roses unnoticed to the floor. I cried out and took off at a dead run—launching myself at the vision before me.*

*He had been leaning indolently against the doorframe of my dressing room—waiting patiently for me to look up from the flowers. I jumped into his arms and wrapped my legs around his waist. He caught and held me without issue, though I could have sworn I heard a small grunt of pain, but I wasn't sure.*

*The very next second, I was sobbing uncontrollably and I couldn't hear anything beyond that.*

I had destroyed my beautiful stage makeup crying all over Sage. I couldn't wrap my head around the fact that he was alive or that I was in his arms. It was a miracle that I thanked God for. And Sage had been in pain and still was, though he wouldn't admit it.

With all that occurred, that moment felt forever ago, but in reality it was yesterday. So I hoped this forced seclusion would allow Sage time to recuperate from his gunshot wounds.

I couldn't think too long about our months of separation, without a pain so deep that it took my breath away. Horrible months when Sage was—*dead*: forever beyond the touch of my fingers, the graze of my lips.

Deaf to my whispered, *I love you*'s.

Just gone!

That visceral connection had felt severed, like a void never to be refilled and a pain forever unrelieved.

I turned into Sage's kiss and poured all my love into it. I rejoiced as he took the kiss deeper; arousing my heart and my soul, while tempering the painful, yet reminiscent grief that still ghosted through me. He slowly decreased the heat of his kiss, but pulled me tighter into him.

"Let's sleep. I'm exhausted and of no use to you at this point," he chuckled, "Except as, perhaps, a heating blanket."

I could hear the fatigue in his voice, and I knew that he must truly need the rest. I snuggled deep into the covers and into the protection and warmth of his body.

A few minutes later his breathing evened out into deep sleep. His absolute trust and vulnerability in this moment was humbling. I vowed I would protect him too, no matter what. I might not have his physical strength, but I could protect him in other ways.

Our relationship had been anything but normal. From how we met, to how we fell in love—it had been high adrenaline and high emotion from the start.

But I wouldn't change a thing. Or *almost* nothing. I could do without the kidnapping, the rape, and the killing of Natalia, my cousin. Yet, had some of those things not happened, I might not have met Sage.

I couldn't even contemplate a life without him.

I'd done that once before and it had sucked! I'd thrown that painful t-shirt away.

"You're thinking so loud, you woke me up," Sage teased, half-awake.

I looked back at him to apologize and stuttered in awe. The light from the fireplace was bathing us in a soft glow and when he smiled that endearing, crooked smile at me, it caused his dimple to wink at me from his left cheek. God, he was beautiful to me!

"I know. I'm sorry," I said a bit breathlessly, "I got to thinking about one thing and it led to twenty others. I'm done now. I promise. Let's get some sleep."

Turning, I rested under his arm and snuggled up to his side with my head pillowed on his chest. The cadence of his heart lulled me quickly to sleep. I felt safe and secure in that moment. If only the feeling would have lasted forever.

# CHAPTER TWO

# Ava

After the first couple of days we settled into a comfortable rhythm. Lazy mornings eating breakfast in bed and making love until we fell back to sleep wrapped in peace. Afternoons spent exploring the wilderness around the rustic cabin; for pleasure, but as Sage explained, for a precaution as well—just in case we were forced to leave.

Moments of love interspersed with stark reminders that we were still in danger and couldn't take our safety for granted. Even secluded in the mountains, as we were, the threat was ever-present.

Our evenings were spent sharing childhood memories, often while cuddled together in the cozy sleigh bed. We wanted to know everything there was to know about one another. Conversations that were free of artifice and often raw with emotion.

I loved to listen to Sage's deep, husky voice as he narrated the stories of his life. During those quiet moments together, I had come to recognize the subtle emotions that were woven through each story. I would listen intently for what he said and for what he didn't—while my fingers unconsciously traced the puckered evidence of his mortality.

If we had been denied the opportunity to experience these moments together—now that would have been a tragedy.

Our connection might have been born from a point of darkness, but it didn't matter to us. We had fallen into love—hard and fast during our short time together. But instead of flaming out just as fast, we had forged a bond that felt inseparable.

We were surrounded in a bubble of love and contentment. The beautifully restored cabin and the picturesque mountains were our paradise and I had no desire to ever leave.

During our talks we discovered that we had a lot in common, though on the surface you wouldn't think so. Sage had been raised by his grandparents, and I had been raised by my adoptive mother. Neither of us had known our biological mothers.

His mother had taken off for Europe after he'd been born and never returned to LA. My mother, Grace Leclair, and her parents died in a car accident when I was three. Her best friend Chole DeLaney had adopted me.

Chloe had loved me as if I were her very own daughter. As far as I was concerned, not only was she my mother, but she was my best friend. I missed Maman something fierce. She had died last year after a long battle with cancer.

We were raised without our fathers. But Sage had a father figure that he loved and respected in his grandfather. And I had Mason and Daniel for brothers. Though recently, I had been reunited with my father, Alexei. We'd been getting to know one another when Sage and I had to flee LA and hide in the safety of the mountains.

***

Sage gradually increased his activities around the cabin as he recovered from his gunshot wounds. After a month or so I wouldn't have known that he had ever been injured. Except for the lingering evidence I saw every day—the puckered red scars marring his otherwise smooth chest.

As his recovery progressed, we adjusted our routine. Each day at noon, Sage and I would go for a walk around the property. We would meet on the front porch after spending the late morning doing our own thing. I usually danced in the cabin and he did activities outside. Or ran into town for supplies.

When I came out of the cabin to greet Sage, he wasn't waiting for me as usual.

"Sage?" I called out, thinking he must be close by.

He didn't answer me with words, but I heard what sounded suspiciously like a lumberjack. I shook my head at the crazy man. He was supposed to be resting.

I found Sage at the back of the cabin chopping wood.

Mesmerized, I watched as he swung the ax from over his left shoulder to split the log in half. And then in half again. His long dark hair hung across his forehead and kept getting into his blue eyes. Impatiently he shook his head to move the errant strands out of his vision.

His swing was rhythmic and efficient, never missing a beat. Or so it seemed. But I knew him well and could see the slight hitch in his swing. Heard the grunt of pain —though barely vocalized.

"Look at you, Mr. Lumberjack. That's a ton of wood," I said, looking at the pile of wood Sage had chopped while I'd been dancing.

"Well, technically it's only about a quarter of a cord. So more like half a ton, instead of an actual ton." He suppressed his laughter.

"Well, technically we are supposed to be on our walk. Are we still going? Because if not, I could always look through those boxes we found stored in the closet." I said eager to look through them.

Sage already knew that I was going to start rummaging through those boxes of untold mysteries. I was in search of hidden treasures. We knew the boxes were just his grandparents' belongings. But I had plans to organize them for Sage and save the things that he might want to keep.

A few of the boxes contained pictures from the surrounding area. I couldn't wait to check those out. Sage told me to feel free to purge things, but I wouldn't throw anything away until he had looked them over first. It wouldn't feel right.

"Is it that time already?" He asked—surprised, "Yeah, let's go. You're not getting out of it," Sage teased, as he grabbed a bottled water and chugged it in one long swallow.

And I just about swallowed my tongue watching the muscles of his neck work as he drained it. He didn't even have to try and I was all worked up. I turned away in an attempt to gain control over my wayward hormones. I wanted to rush over and jump on him and to hell with the walk.

"Are you up for a more advanced hike, Beauty? There's a special place I'd like to take you to. I was thinking we could hike there today."

"I'd love to see it. Let me grab the backpack and some lunch," I said as I turned and walked back into the cabin.

When I returned, Sage was ready to go. I followed him to the trail that was behind the cabin, Sage carrying the pack. He said that the trail was strenuous, but manageable. It led up the mountain behind us.

The first part of our hike was made in comfortable silence, as we concentrated on our footing along the overgrown trail. We had been hiking for about thirty minutes and I was definitely feeling the incline. But it felt good to work up a sweat and utilize different muscles than what I used when dancing.

"How much further do you think?" I asked as we stopped for a water break.

Pointing to the head of the trail, Sage replied, "See how the vegetation thins out at the top?"

I nodded my head that I did.

"We're headed in that direction. Maybe ten minutes."

I continued to follow along, taking in the flowers, the wildlife, and the distant mountains that were playing peek-a-boo through the pine trees. My heart was pounding a little more than was necessary for the incline at this point. I took several deep breaths in and out to calm myself as we started to crest the top of the trail.

Sage was ahead of me now by about fifty feet. I slowed my pace and wiped the wetness off my cold, clammy hands and onto my jeans. I closed my eyes.

Nope, I opened them swiftly. That didn't help.

By the time I stopped walking, I stood a few feet from Sage and was at the top of the trailhead.

Hyperventilating, I looked forward and then down. Huge mistake. We were standing on a precipice and there was a rocky gorge below us—only a few feet away from my booted toes.

"It's just over there, Beauty," Sage said, as he pointed off to the right, then turned and walked in that direction. "My ledge overlooks the beautiful valley below. It's like sitting on a sofa and watching the wildlife channel."

Paralyzed, I couldn't move. I couldn't call out his name. Fear had stolen my capacity to speak.

# CHAPTER THREE

# Sage

It had been well over a year since I had last snuck away to my mountains. Working undercover didn't lend itself to a regular life with scheduled vacations and such. I still managed to drive here a few times a year to decompress, regardless of life circumstances.

The natural rock formation that I discovered with my grandfather years ago was nestled into the side the mountain. We would sit on our rocky sofa and look out over the valley below and to the mountain ranges beyond. Even as an active young boy, I could appreciate the beauty of the forests and the wildlife inhabiting them.

"I could sit here all day," I told Ava, as I took in the beauty before me. Absorbed in the view, it was a few minutes before I realized that Ava hadn't joined me on the ledge. I looked over my shoulder to where she had stopped a few minutes ago.

"Ava!" I jumped up and ran over to her—alarmed by her pallor. "What's wrong? Are you ill?"

Her skin was a pale shade of green and her dilated pupils were crowding her silver irises. She looked ready to puke or to faint in fear.

"Ava?" She wouldn't look at me and continued to stare at the valley below—transfixed. I picked her up to cradle her in my arms and carried her to my rock sofa.

"Talk to me, Ava. You're scaring me." I begged, as I stroked her face, her arms, and picked up her clammy hands to hold in mine.

"I...I'm afraid of heights," she whispered before burying her face against my shoulder.

I stood up and quickly carried her away. Once back down the trail and away from the ledge, I sat on a boulder and faced the sun. I hated that I didn't know every little detail about her. Like her fear of heights.

"Ava, I'm so sorry," I said, kissing her gently in apology.

"It's not your fault." She whispered, her voice still tight with fear. "I thought that perhaps I would have grown out of it by now." She shook her head, more for herself than for me, and said, "apparently not."

"Hey, now. There's no shame in having a fear of heights. I just wish that I had known. We could've approached this hike a bit differently."

"I don't know why I'm so afraid of heights. I just know that I have been for as long as I can remember."

Ava told me how as a child, she had rarely ventured out of the desert community where she lived. Palm Springs was nestled in a valley that was less than five hundred feet above sea level. It was surrounded and protected on all four sides by various mountain ranges.

The one and only time she had ventured out of the valley and up into the mountains had been with Mason and Daniel for a school field trip. They had taken The

Palm Springs Aerial Tramway up the side of Mount San Jacinto.

"I didn't enjoy it. Not one bit. Mainly because that's when I discovered I was afraid of heights. A total scaredy-cat. I had become so nauseous on the ride up. I thought I must have eaten something bad. Once we were almost to the top, I thought my heart would explode out of my chest. It felt as if I would suddenly fall over the edge or jump over the stupid thing of my own volition—and crash to my death on the rocks below."

She told me that our trip up to the mountains had been a much better experience. Basically because it had been dark and she had slept most of the way. Plus, we had arrived in a car and not a little tram traveling two-and-a-half miles up the side of a mountain, swinging from a cable high above the rocky gorge below.

"No, thank you!"

I laughed, I couldn't help it.

Luckily we were still sitting, so I grabbed her firmly by the back of the head and I kissed her hard. Trying to absorb all of her fear and give her my compassion in return.

Turning in my arms, Ava straddled my hips and we took the kiss deeper. Our tongues dueled and our teeth nipped as we expressed our rising passions. Bathed in the warm sun and surrounded by nature's beauty, it was a moment of true perfection. One that I would store away to recall and relive.

"I love you, Beauty," I said, as I gentled the kiss. "Maybe we should go back down to the cabin and have some lunch."

Ava looked at me as if I had lost my mind and maybe I had.

"Why do you think you are so afraid of heights?"

"I don't really know. It has just always been there. But I didn't appreciate how much it affected me until I was on that field trip with Mason and Daniel. They could see that I was freaking out. Mason held me against his chest and I kept my eyes closed most of the way. We were so young, but even then they protected me like brothers."

Jealousy, fast and unreasonable, flashed through me. I had no right to covet the relationship that she shared with them, but I couldn't deny that I did.

"Maman and I never really discussed it. She knew I was afraid and we left it at that. She had little quirks and figured this was just one of mine. But the next time I had a field trip scheduled for the tram, I stayed home with Maman. She understood perfectly and didn't press me to go," Ava said with a shrug.

I wanted to know why. I wanted to fix it. I wanted to be her hero—past, present, and always.

# CHAPTER FOUR

# Ava

"On second thought, instead of going home, there's another place I'd like to show you," Sage told me, as he headed down the trail.

I followed slowly behind him, as the aftereffects of fear were still coursing through me. I had to navigate the trail on shaking legs.

Sage stopped at a meadow-like area that was nestled in among the pine trees. He knelt down to spread out a blanket that I had placed into the pack.

"Come here, Beauty," he beckoned me as I walked towards him, "let's have some lunch and enjoy the sunshine."

"What a perfect idea."

I sat next Sage and watched as he pulled the sandwiches and the grapes out of the pack for us to enjoy. Now that fear had loosened its hold over me—the *crash* from the fight-or-flight response had left me shakier and ravenously hungry.

We ate in companionable silence while enjoying the warm sunshine. But now that I was full and no longer shaking, I was ready for a little nap and I told Sage as such.

"Let's stretch out for a bit. I could do with one too," he told me, as we laid down together, side-by-side.

Sage pulled me in close to him, wrapping his arms around me. It didn't take me long to fall asleep at all. Thankfully, there were no nightmares waiting to greet me once my eyes were closed.

I was drifting, buoyant on warm sunshine and the scent of wildflowers tickling my nose. Slowly opening my eyes, I was greeted by the bright blue sky captured within Sage's gaze.

"I wondered if you'd ever wake up, sleepy-head," he said, looking down at me with a mischievous grin gracing his full lips and devilry in his eyes.

Held within his fingertips was the source of my wildflower scent. I drew in the heady fragrance as Sage feathered my cheek and neck with the soft yellow petals.

"That tickles," I said giggling.

"Does this tickle?" He asked, as he drew the flower across my bottom lip.

A shuddering breath escaped from between my parted lips. My tongue peeked out to wet them and my teeth scraped along my bottom lip to ease the tingling sensation.

Sage lowered his head to mine and captured my wet bottom lip with his kiss. Sweet and gentle was how he sipped at my mouth—languishing over every facet of his kiss.

"So beautiful, Ava. Flushed from the sun and from my kisses."

I didn't have time to respond, as Sage came back for more. This time taking his kiss deeper—but slow and thorough.

With his left hand he stroked down my neck and along my delicate collar bone. He fingered the edge of my blue v-neck sweater, pulling it over to expose my shoulder.

His lips followed the same path as his fingers, anointing my skin and leaving a trail of heat.

"I love when you do that," I told him, as he ran his hand through my long chestnut hair.

"Your hair is magnificent. Long and thick."

He brought a handful to his nose and drew in a large breath. Such a simple thing, but so completely arousing. The look in his eyes told me all I needed to know about how he was affected.

Sage came at my mouth again. This time he dove in and drove me hard. Nibbling and sucking at my lips and my tongue, until I was panting for breath and ready to flip him over and rip off his clothes.

"Let me see you bathed in nothing but sunlight, Ava."

We helped each other to undress, which included lots of kissing, touching, and exploring. The day was warm with only the slightest chill to the air, but I didn't expect that to be a problem for long.

Finally, we were left wearing nothing but sunshine.

Sage gathered me into his arms and laid me down. Resting on his elbow, he looked me over from head to toe. His gaze warming me faster than the sun could ever hope to.

He lifted my left hand to his mouth and kissed the skin just above my engagement ring.

"I love you, Ava DeLaney." Love and passion evident in his husky voice.

"I love you more, Sage Cartier," I teased, but meant with absolute sincerity.

I couldn't speak after that, as Sage was busy making love to every part of me. My heart had been first and foremost to receive his attention with his declaration of love. But the rest quickly followed suit.

When his lips and teeth made their way to my breasts, I moaned aloud despite being out in the open and under the wide blue sky. But I felt safe and secure with the trees acting as sentinels to our private sanctuary.

My hands threaded through Sage's dark hair. Gripping and pulling him closer to my breasts as I arched my back for him.

"Yes, Sage, just like that," I encouraged, as he took my nipple deep into his hungry mouth.

He wrapped his right hand under my back, but still propped up on his elbow and pulled me closer. His left hand cupped my right breast as he continued to attend to my left one with his mouth.

He let loose of my nipple and the cool air was the perfect contrast to the heated, distended tip.

"So beautiful how you respond to me," he crooned, as he made his way to my abdomen.

My muscles quivered with the anticipation of where he was going. Just the memory of how his talented mouth could send me over was almost enough to have me exploding with an orgasm before he even had the chance to touch me.

Sage positioned himself between my legs and pushed my knees wide. He looked at me with his beautiful blue eyes, letting me see his passion and his love. He dipped his head, still watching me, and ran the flat of his tongue over my engorged clitoris. My hips bucked uncontrollably.

He alternated licking at my clitoris and flicking it with his stiffened tongue. He continued to watch me—our eyes locked in passion. I held his gaze as long as I could, but when the sensations became too overwhelming and too intense, I closed my eyes and got lost in just feeling.

I threw my head back and screamed out a guttural sound as I crashed through my first orgasm.

Sage added his fingers next to layer the intensity of the sensations and brought me to another level of passion. Which in turn caused another, even more intense orgasm. I was a quivering mess, yet begged for more.

"God! Sage, please."

He knew exactly what I was begging for. I wanted to feel every glorious inch of him filling me to perfection.

He leaned forward and kissed me ravenously. I tasted myself in his kiss and he deepened it, as need swept through us like a tsunami.

Propped up on his palms, Sage positioned himself at my entrance, but didn't seat himself within me. He swept his gaze up and down my body.

"Look at you, Beauty. All flushed pink with your passion and arousal," he said, as he rubbed his thumb along my bottom lip, dislodging it from between teeth and inserting his thumb into my mouth.

I bit at the pad of his thumb. I tongued and sucked on it, knowing that he would love it if I did so.

He centered his gaze on where we were about to be joined. I followed his lead, leaning up on my elbows so that I could watch too. My breath caught when he started to press forward, slowly filling me with his length and his girth.

I lifted my hips.

"Perfect." Sage moaned, as he slowly, but inextricably pressed forward—stretching me to accommodate his size.

"You are not stopping this time," I said, or begged, "please, Sage. Move!"

"Okay, love, no stopping this time."

And he made good on his word.

As soon as he had reached the end of me, he pressed in deeper with the flex of his gloriously tight ass and a thrust of his hips. My breath caught as the pain-pleasure threshold became one and the same.

His hips were a slow and steady piston. Back and forth with no stopping. Working me towards another, fast approaching orgasm.

I laid back down, as I could no longer support myself on my arms. I was all toe-curling sensation. Sage hooked his arms around my knees, spreading them high and wide, and then let loose of his prized control.

As per usual, nothing of intelligence spilled from my mouth. I babbled incoherencies that I knew Sage would tease me about later.

"Oh. God. Oh. God Oh. God." Was about all that I could manage when I crested what I thought was the final explosive orgasm.

Sage slowed his pace, a gentle back and forth that allowed me to recover. "One more Ava, then I'll go with you."

I wasn't sure I had another one in me; however, yet again, Sage proved to me that I did. But this time he went with me.

"I love you, Beauty," he grunted out, as we came together under the beautiful fall sky.

He lay down beside me and pulled me to him. I was wrapped securely in his arms and his love. He draped his jacket over us, as our skin began to cool.

"I love you, Sage. That was beyond words." I kissed his lips softly in thanks, but he added his residual passion to the kiss, stoking the fires again.

I could feel his engorged erection pressing against my hip, so I wiggled them, signaling to Sage I was game for more.

Tilting my hips back with an arch of my back, we stayed on our sides, but Sage entered me from behind. With my legs together, it was a snug fit, but Sage managed it with a little wiggling on my part.

He slid in and out, slow and methodical. Never speeding up or slowing down, just a slow ride to our climactic finish. Holding my breasts in both of his hands, Sage pulled and plucked at my distended nipples. A perfect counterpoint to how his cock stimulated my vaginal walls. Pain and pleasure—well balanced and to heighten my pleasure and amplify my orgasm.

With a quick stroke of my clitoris I was exploding and Sage came again with me.

I was beyond sleepy now and fell straight to sleep or passed out, whatever you want to call it. I didn't even say I love you to Sage. Hopefully, he had fallen asleep too.

But when I fell asleep this time, it was to fall straight into my nightmares—with no transition whatsoever. No preparation for the pain and degradation that I would feel, but wouldn't remember. And no way to escape or fight back against the shadows ripping me apart and destroying my soul.

Gripping hands shook me. I screamed in terror and scrambled to escape.

# CHAPTER FIVE

# Ava

*Darling Sage,*

*I have never stopped longing for you or for the love that we shared. That kind of connection only comes once in a lifetime and you were it for me. I should have never walked away from you and that kind of love. Pray forgive my blind ambition and my youthful ignorance as to what was important. I should have never chosen my career and social standing over you.*

I glanced down and then quickly away from the small box that sat tauntingly at my feet. The porch swing swayed back and forth—the movement doing nothing to soothe my inner turmoil.

I looked out over the mountaintop paradise and reminisced over the past three months with Sage. The picturesque scenery had come at a high price.

My freedom. But to be fair, Sage's too.

I could see for miles away and allowed myself to be lost within the landscape before me, instead of lost in my internal one. Fall had crept quietly across the mountains; seemingly between one day and the next.

I continued to ignore that little box screaming at me.

The forests were lush with evergreen. The meadows were teeming with multicolored wildflowers and the sun was shining from an unbelievably blue sky. If I only had a talent for painting, I would have captured this moment to save forever.

I lifted my iPhone and quickly snapped a photo just as an orphaned cloud floated by. I kept trying to duplicate the view, but technology couldn't compete with nature's vibrant colors and subtle hues.

It would have been a beautiful, idyllic utopia if not for the cloistered feeling that had started pressing down upon me. I was chaffing at the confinement and the lack of freedom, and paradise was starting to feel like prison. And we shouldn't be the ones in jail.

I wasn't allowed to talk with the locals. Not that I would have the opportunity to in any case, as Sage always went to town by himself. He didn't want them to realize that he wasn't alone at the cabin.

I wasn't allowed to call anyone in LA either. Sage worried that the call might be traced to me and our location. I fully understood and respected the precautions we were taking. The idea of being caught by Ivan again caused fear and revulsion to flash through me and I shivered with dread. I knew that things would not go as well for me next time.

Intellectually, I understood that we were still in danger, but three months was a long time to be absent from life.

I missed my best friends, Mason and Daniel. We had been fairly inseparable since we were kids. They had both left Palm Springs to attend USC. I had stayed home to care for my adoptive mother fighting a losing battle with cancer.

The three of us had been separated by the desert that was Palm Springs and an endless concrete jungle. But we had managed to remain close by texting and chatting on the phone frequently. My new friends, Willow and Riley, were like the sisters I had always dreamt of having. I missed them more than I thought I would.

To keep from going stir crazy these past few months I kept myself busy by dancing in the mornings. The wood floors in the cabin were perfect for ballet. And since there wasn't much furniture, I would move what pieces there were to the edges of the room and out of my way. The morning light that flooded the cabin while I danced was perfect—soft and touched with magic.

Sage and I still went hiking, though we avoided the areas with steep ledges and drop-offs. Luckily there were no repeats of my episode by the rocky sofa. Or another nightmare like the one after we had made love under the wide blue sky.

Sage had questioned me about my nightmares, but I didn't want to talk about them. Besides, I couldn't remember any details. I wouldn't share the terror and pain I felt. It would make him feel helpless and perhaps make him feel as if he had failed me. Which was ridiculous.

So we had left it for now, though he didn't like that. I was afraid the nightmares were beyond his help, or mine for that matter. They would just have to run their course. Or I could just keep ignoring them as much as possible.

*Dreams,* as Dr. Wong called them, were trying to tell me something. But what?

When I wasn't dancing or hanging out with Sage, I sorted through the boxes that we found stored in the cabin. They were like little time capsules and they helped to occupy my mind away from my forced confinement.

Scattered through the various boxes were older photos taken of the surrounding area. They illustrated how much the forest had matured over the years. I set the best ones aside. I was planning to do a framed series of forest photos—contrasting then and now—as a gift for Sage.

The pictures of Sage's grandparents, Pete and Winnie, were my favorite. The love they had for each other had shone brightly in every picture taken of the two of them together. Her head leaning towards him, as if she couldn't get close enough. He appeared to be just as magnetic as his grandson.

My thoughts returned to that damned box and that damned letter—just as they had all day, every day since I had discovered it last week. I wished that I hadn't found it. The letter had been nestled innocuously within a box of pictures and had been addressed to, *Darling Sage.*

I glanced down at my engagement ring as jealousy ate at my heart.

I thought back to the night Sage had slipped his ring onto my finger. Fearing for my life, we had fled LA for this mountain hideaway. My cousin, Natalia, had saved my life and in the process had lost hers. I had tried to keep my shit together as we drove to our destination, but too much had happened.

I couldn't stand to be in the car for one moment longer and begged Sage to stop. We ended up at the beach so we could stretch our legs.

We had been walking for a bit, when Sage had suddenly dropped to his knees on the sand. While kneeling on the beach before me and under a benevolent moon, Sage had asked me to be his wife. It had been incredibly moving and beautiful, despite the danger that Ivan had presented.

*Darling Sage,* floated through my mind again—for like the thousandth time since I had first read it.

Of course I realized that Sage had known and loved other women before me. But I didn't have to like it. And I didn't. Not at all.

Having the written evidence in my hands had made it all too tangible. So I'd dropped the letter back into the box where I found it, then tossed a handful of pictures on top of it to hide the evidence from Sage and from myself.

I walked away and attempted to forget her opening declaration. But out of sight was not out of mind. Ignoring my conscience, as it nagged at me to tell Sage, was not as easy as I had thought it would be.

I could run from the danger back in LA to hide in the mountains, but I couldn't run from myself or the effects of those few words.

*Darling Sage.*

The regret this woman had felt and the love that she had expressed for Sage were evident and too painful to read.

A week later and I still hadn't found the courage to finish reading her words.

Who was this woman? Would Sage want to rekindle things with her? Was it too late for that? Was it ever too late? People changed their minds all the time. We were a throw-away society these days.

My heart ached and my head spun with chaotic indecision.

I felt like my paradise had been lost, hijacked by the ink pressed upon that lonely page.

# CHAPTER SIX

# Ava

The next morning was Monday, so Sage had driven in to town for more groceries and to use the phone at the store to call his Lieut. Mondays were his day to report in and receive updates on the investigation.

Unfortunately, not much had changed in that regard during the months that we had been away. Sage told me that they were no closer to finding Ivan. And there had been numerous leads pursued, but so far none of those had resulted in his capture.

While he was away in town, I spent the morning dancing harder and longer than I usually did. I hoped to alleviate the angst consuming me and this uncomfortable, yet misplaced anger I had towards Sage. Unfair of me, but there it was.

I felt infused with a painful sadness that I couldn't name. I knew I was being ridiculous, like a child having a tantrum, but I couldn't shake jealousy's hold over me.

I had just finished dancing for the morning when I stormed over to the box where the letter sat, mocking me. I snatched the letter out of the box and walked with determined strides out the front door.

I leaned against the porch railing and snapped the letter open in a fit of pissyness. I was angry with myself for turning this letter into an albatross that was all but choking me.

*Darling Sage,*

*I have never stopped longing for you or for the love that we shared. That kind of connection only comes once in a lifetime and you were it for me. I should have never walked away from you and that kind of love. Pray forgive my blind ambition and my youthful ignorance as to what was important. I should have never chosen my career and social standing over you.*

*Sage, I've paid the ultimate price. An unbearable price that can never be undone or rectified, no matter how much I atone for it. I will spend the rest of my life doing so, though that may not be for long.*

I stopped reading. Honestly it was no more palatable the second time around. However, the letter was not continuing in the direction that I thought it would.

Who was this woman and what was she talking about? In the beginning she spoke so eloquently about her love and longing for Sage. But now she describes a pain that practically resonated off the page. I wasn't sure that I wanted to read any more. But I felt I had no choice. I felt compelled to reach the end. I wanted to understand this woman and her message.

*Sage, after I married Brent and became a Deputy District Attorney, I was on the fast track and rising faster. You had been away undercover when I headed up an LAPD investigation into the criminal activity of Alexei Vinokourov.*

I gasped out loud and looked to see if Sage had returned from town, but I didn't see him. I walked over to the porch swing and sat down taking a deep breath to collect myself. I quickly flipped the letter to the last page to see who had written it. The name Tomi Delacourt was signed across the bottom.

I began to reread her words with a new mindset and a sigh of relief. I may not know everything there was to know about Tomi Delacourt, but from what Sage had said, she went missing over five years ago and was presumed to be dead. Now her words took on an ominous tone and I shivered as I read the words penned by a ghost.

*Sage, I'm not sure if you remember that Brent worked for a large securities corporation as their head IT guy. Brent loved to tinker on the computer and was quite brilliant at it. When I told him about our investigation of Alexei, he took it upon himself to do a thorough investigation using an untraceable computer. He didn't tell me what he was doing. But when he finally confessed, he had compiled quite a bit of information. This information led us in a direction we could have never predicted nor foreseen. Ultimately, I feel it led to his death and to the death of my little Emma.*

She had kept saying Sage's name, as if begging for forgiveness. A teardrop landed on the page I was reading. I couldn't even imagine what it would feel like for a mother to lose a child, especially when you felt you were somehow responsible. I couldn't fathom that kind of pain. And in the face of these words and the anguish that was evident, I felt ridiculous for being consumed by jealousy over the past week.

*Sage, with this letter you will find a flash drive that contains all the information that Brent had inadvertently found. It's for this information that Brent and Emma died and the fault is all mine. I was too blind to what was important and too greedy for the DA's office to see what the ultimate price would be. And who would have to pay it.*

I stopped reading and ran into the house to look through the box where I had found the letter. Kneeling down, I rummaged through the contents looking for the flash drive. I found it at the bottom in the corner. I kept searching to make sure that it was the only one. Too intent to move, I stayed kneeling as I continued the letter.

*I lost my family. I lost my career. I'll probably lose my life.*

*But not before I pass along this information to you, because I know without a doubt that you will make these men pay and justice will be served. For Brent and for my Emma.*

*Sage, take the flash drive to a secure computer and open the file named, The Dark. It's an encrypted file and you need a pass code to get into it. The pass code is the day, the month, and the year that we went to Griffith Observatory on our first date. What Brent found is beyond the scope of the LAPD. It's beyond your scope, but I have faith*

*in your ability to find the right person to give this informa-*
*tion to.*

*Sage, it's more than   the trafficking of drugs, small*
*arms, and humans. So watch your back, but more impor-*
*tantly, be careful who you trust. I'm leaving this informa-*
*tion with grandpa Pete for when you get back from your*
*undercover assignment. I'll be long gone or long dead, but*
*please remember, Sage, I never stopped loving you.*

"Sage! Sage!" I started screaming when I heard Sage slam the car door shut. He needed to read this letter from Tomi.

I felt sick for having kept this information to myself over the past week. Had I but known, I would've handed the letter over when I found it. I prayed he would forgive me for my petty jealousies.

# CHAPTER SEVEN

# Ava

It felt like we arrived back to LA in a blur of scenery, streaking down the mountain at warp speed and into unknown danger.

The trip home had mirrored our trip away and yet, the danger looming over us felt stronger and thicker than it had before we had fled LA in the first place. Sage was quiet, so I followed suit. I wanted to know where we were going, but I didn't want to be the first one to break the silence.

I thought back to yesterday when I had screamed for Sage. He had snuck into the cabin with his gun drawn. I was a little taken aback, but in retrospect I had probably scared the hell out of him.

Seriously Ava, what did you think the man was going to do, come strolling around the corner whistling a tune of nonchalance? I shook my head. I felt bad for alarming him. He was worried about my safety, first and foremost. I would do well to remember that...

Responding to my cry, Sage had silently crept in through the back door of the cabin. He grabbed me swiftly and shoved my back hard against an interior wall, then placed his body flush against mine. He was a wall of flesh protecting the front of me and the cabin wall protecting the back of me. The letter and the flash drive had fallen to the floor in the process.

"What is it? Did you see someone?" He whispered urgently into my ear.

The breath had been knocked out of me, so I didn't answer straight away. He had his gun up and at the ready. His head whipped back and forth to look out to the front cabin and then the back where he had come from. He was hyper vigilant and searching for whatever had threatened me and caused me to yell out.

"Sage. Sage, I'm okay." I reached up with my hand to cradle the side of his face. Gently I turned him towards me. "Look at me, please. I'm so terribly sorry. I was reading this letter that had been addressed to you and Sage..." I looked him straight in the eyes and hoped that mine conveyed my remorse and empathy.

But before I could take a breath to continue, Sage had tucked his gun into the back of his pants and pushed me against the wall. I shivered as a chill of foreboding worked its way down my spine, but before I could put much thought into it, Sage was devouring my mouth with aggressive passion.

His rush of adrenaline had morphed into a rush of heat that I both acknowledged and welcomed. His lips, his tongue, and his teeth made quick work of mine and I was on fire within moments. He worked his way from my mouth to my cheek and then kissed his way along my jawline. Biting gently at the side of my neck.

He told me through his actions how scared he had been for me and for us, and yet how upset he was for my silence. As his mouth was busy worshipping me, his hands were busy removing my dance clothes until I stood naked before him.

Sage stepped back and looked me over with his electric blue eyes. Glowing with passion, they spoke eloquently of what was to come. My breath caught in my throat as I watched him unfasten his jeans and pull out his erection. Two steps forward and he was grabbing me about my hips and lifting me up and back against the wall. He nestled his cock against my weeping entrance and with one quick thrust he was seated as far as he could go.

And stopped.

The need for him to move was overwhelming. So I gripped him tight internally. I had learned over the past three months that in doing so was guaranteed to bring Sage closer to the edge.

"You scared me half to death." he said, as he leaned forward to devour my mouth. This pushed him further into me, just shy of uncomfortable. A throaty moan of pleasure rumbled through his chest. Reaching down between my widespread legs with his left hand, Sage began working my clitoris making sure that I went over first.

It wouldn't take long.

"I'm sorry, Beauty, this is going to be a quick one." He told me as his hips started a gentle in and out that rapidly quickened in pace.

"Let me feel you. Please don't hold back. I won't break." I begged.

Leaning forward I bit into his bottom lip. This prompted the desired effect and Sage dropped his prized control. I could feel the difference between when he held the reins too tight and when he finally let them go. It was then that his passion became unbridled. It wouldn't be long before I was orgasming like a brilliant supernova; all light and no substance.

I exploded and called out Sage's name. He quickly followed, waiting for me to go first. God, I loved him with every fiber of who I was. And I was his—plain and simple.

He was seated deep and holding still. So I tightened rhythmically on his still hardened cock eliciting moans from both of us and a fresh round of thrusts. I quickly came again. Afterwards Sage lowered my legs and held me tight.

He kissed me deeply before picking up my ballet clothes and handing them to me. I went to the bathroom to clean up and redress. When I returned, Sage had his back to me and was facing the front door.

I walked up from behind to wrap my arms around him, then told him the news I had been dreading for over a week, "It was from Tomi," I finally said.

"What?" he said, as he stepped forward and away from me, leaving me cold.

"Tomi wrote me a letter? And it was here at the cabin?"

"Yes. Grandpa Pete must have brought it up here. I found it in a box of photos I was looking through—last week." I hadn't wanted to admit that last part, but it only seemed fair to tell him the whole truth.

He walked out the front door and on to the porch without a backwards glance. I could see through the window that he had sat down on the swing.

After what we had just shared I had no right to feel hurt, but I couldn't deny the fact that jealousy was a close friend. I was feeling like second choice—to a ghost. I notched up my chin and walked straight out the front door and sat down on the swing too.

Sage was quiet as he read through Tomi's letter for a second time. He lowered the letter and stared down at the flash drive resting in his hand.

Would we have to leave our mountain paradise? And while I had been itching to return to my life as it were, I wouldn't have chosen to return in this manner.

"Why didn't you tell me?" He asked quietly, as he lifted his gaze to look out over the mountains.

I could feel his confusion as he tried to figure out why I would keep this information from him and to myself. Honestly, I couldn't say for certain. All I knew with any certainty was that jealousy had gripped my heart and wouldn't let go.

Gripped it still.

"Sage, I'm so sorry. I have no excuses. Truth be told, I didn't even read the letter in its entirety until today. I had read the first paragraph and that had been enough. I couldn't bring myself to read any further."

Sage still wouldn't look at me, so I hurried to finish explaining the inexplicable.

"It was painfully obvious to me that whoever had written that letter was still in love with you. So I put it away. Out of sight, out of mind. Or so I had thought. But, it hadn't worked out the way I had planned. Those words had taunted me all week until I couldn't stand it anymore." I paused a moment to collect myself as various emotions assailed me.

"Once I shook off the jealousy that had diverted my reasoning, I read the letter again. But this time, I read it all the way through and with a different perspective."

"She knew she was in serious trouble, Sage. I don't profess to understand what's going on. But Tomi clearly felt that whatever information had been uncovered ultimately lead to her family being murdered."

I felt tears slide down my face as I thought of the pain that had resonated from those pages. Did he feel it too? The confusion and the remorse?

I wanted to comfort him and in doing so comfort myself. Because for the first time, I felt a distance between us. And within that gap was a ghostly sentinel awaiting justice for the deaths of her husband and her little girl.

How could he walk away from that? He couldn't.

I knew he wouldn't.

She appealed to Sage's needs and perfectly so. To protect and to serve the innocent. How could I possibly compete with that? Not that I wanted to, but damn a girl wanted to feel and know that she was front and center in her man's world.

"Ava," Sage had finally said, as he turned to look at me. "Come here, Beauty, I want to hold you."

And just like that I felt like a two-year-old for my mental tantrum and yet, I felt precious all the same. He was turning to me for the same comfort that I was seeking in him.

I crawled into Sage's lap and we sat that way for some time. We held onto one another until we grew comfortable with each other again and regained that sense of peace. Sage seemed to intuitively know what it was that I needed. I buried my flaming-red face against his neck in an attempt to hide the evidence of my shame.

"Beauty, you do know that I can still see your lovely blush?" he teased. Sage continued, "You know that I'm concerned with your safety and would never do anything to put that into jeopardy. But after reading Tomi's letter we have no choice but to return to LA tomorrow. I need to open that Dark folder and read whatever information Tomi wanted me to have."

He opened his hand so that I could see the flash drive resting ominously on his palm. A specter of unknown danger and consequence.

"I know. Perhaps whatever information Tomi and Brent uncovered will exonerate my father and help to solve their murders. Especially little Emma's. No one should take the life of a child and for that alone, you must find justice." I didn't know this little girl, but her death angered me.

Sage hugged me tight and kissed me softly on the neck just behind my ear. A simple kiss that offered forgiveness and absolution, which was more than I deserved.

The distance between us quickly dissolved as we had made love several more times that night and again the next morning. The residual fullness of his possession was a welcomed reminder as we flew down the mountain towards LA—with danger riding shotgun.

# CHAPTER EIGHT

# Sage

As we drove through LA, I still had no idea where I would ultimately take Ava. She could stay with her father, Alexei. He would love that. Their reunion had been interrupted by our quick departure from the city. I didn't fully trust him, but I knew he loved his daughter. He would jump at the chance to protect his only child and would love to play the hero in her eyes.

Alexei and I had spoken last week when I had made a run into town. He had taken further precautions to secure his Palisades home, all in an effort to protect Ava for when we returned to LA. His home had been compromised and his niece had been shot and killed by Ivan's goon the night of Ava's solo celebration party. He assured me that when Ava came back to town, he would be able to protect her.

Another viable, yet less attractive option was Special Agent Trey Mathieson, FBI. A total prick if there ever was one, but more than capable of keeping Ava safe. I couldn't decide which would be the best solution, as I wanted to be the one to protect Ava.

But short of cutting myself in half, which clearly wasn't an option, I couldn't be in two places at once.

Giving control to someone else, especially as it per-tained to Ava, went against all that I stood for. But I didn't have much of a choice.

I had to solve this mystery for Tomi. I owed it to her memory and to what we had shared. She was the first woman I could imagine spending the rest of my life with, but now there was Ava.

Tomi and I had gone our separate ways to pursue different paths in life, but there was still a lingering sense of nostalgia for what might have been. So in hon-or of that memory, I would do all that I could to solve this on Tomi's behalf.

I pulled my eyes briefly from the road to look over at Ava. She was gazing out the window at downtown LA. I wondered what she was thinking, but hesitated to ask. She'd been quiet on our drive down the mountain, lost to her thoughts. But so had I. Perhaps she was still processing all that had occurred in the last twenty-four hours. I know I was.

That ominous flash drive weighed heavily upon my mind. I had no idea what potential danger I was taking on and for that reason alone, I wouldn't allow Ava to remain with me. At least not until this was all sorted out. I wouldn't trust anyone with this information or at least not until I had investigated the contents of that Dark folder.

I was still in contact with Lieutenant Clarke on Mondays, just like always when I was undercover. He considered this a protective custody assignment be-cause he knew I would have never allowed someone else to watch over Ava. However, with budget cuts there was no way that the LAPD was going to pay me for this assignment, so I had been on administrative leave.

I was due to connect with the Lieut. on Monday next week. Six days away from today. I would reach out to him earlier if I needed to, it would just depend on what I found on the drive and in that Dark folder.

"Sage?" I heard Ava query."Will you tell me where we're going?"

"Well, Beauty, to be honest I have no idea. I can't decide where you would be the safest. In a perfect world I would turn us around and take us back to the mountains to never return. But it's not a perfect world and yet you deserve to live your life free from fear. Free from being relegated to a mountainous prison, albeit a beautiful one."

"Was it that obvious?" she said with a blush.

"Only to me." I told her gently, as I reached out to hold her left hand in mine.

It had only been three months, but I loved to rub my thumb across her engagement ring. I still got a surge of possessiveness every time I saw my ring gracing her finger and when I felt it dragging across my skin—but especially when she gripped my cock tight in her hand.

The ring was the evidence of my ownership.

Of my possession.

She was mine, but I was just as equally hers.

She owned all of me. Heart and soul.

But would she be willing to wait? Would she be willing to sacrifice our near future to solve this mystery from my past? Did she see that I felt I had no choice?

I just hoped that Ava would understand.

# CHAPTER NINE

# Ivan

For the first time in months, Sage Cartier and Ava DeLaney had been spotted in LA. Anticipation was a profound stimulant—intoxicating him almost to distraction.

His team had hacked into the closed circuit video surveillance in and around the city. He had counted on the fact that they would eventually return to LA and prepared for that eventuality.

Cartier's car and license number had been spotted traveling South on the 5. But the facial recognition software running in the background had sealed the deal.

My men would track their progress through the city and once their final destination had been determined, they would let me know.

And then, let the games begin. But for now, there were more important things to focus on.

Tonight was more than just the monthly business meeting. It was the annual reaffirmation ceremony. Preparations for this special evening had started the day after last year's event.

The anticipation for what was to come tonight had him twitching in his seat as he waited for the necessary website to load. And with a few quick keystrokes he accessed the deep web.

Now the evening could truly begin.

The deep web was the invisible part of the internet where he now found himself. It contained more than ninety-nine percent of all of the internet's content. Whereas, the internet that was accessed by the general population and the various search engines like Google, Bing, and Yahoo was known as the surface web.

Those conventional search engines couldn't access or index the deep web, which made it the perfect place to hide cyber crimes.

Once he gained access to the deep web, he opened the Tor encryption browser and entered the URL for the private chat room. This took him to the dark web. A more secretive and highly selective niche within the deep web.

If you knew where to look—anything and everything could be found for hire and for sale within the dark web. He funneled all his *activities* through it and never worried about prying eyes. It was well named and perfectly suited to accomplish the real work of his organization.

For years he had cultivated and utilized the connections he'd made within the deep web. All for the express purpose of advancing himself within the secret society of which he was a member. His efforts had not been in vain and had paid huge dividends. He had become the director of the LA Dark.

The Dark were a society much like the Illuminati, the Bilderberg Group, or the Freemasons—yet not at all. Those groups were talked about incessantly. No one talked about The Dark. No one knew of their existence. Notoriety was not their aim or motivation—anonymity was.

Hiding in plain sight.

The one concession to that anonymity was the dark web—so aptly named after their secret society, The Dark, though no one realized it. The dark web was whispered about with awed tones and had garnered quite the reputation over the years. So the society fanned the rumors and the speculations in hopes of capitalizing on the mystique surrounding the dark web.

The Supremacy, who is the leader of The Dark realized the income potential of the dark web and capitalized on the proliferation of black market activity escalating around the world. His decision had proven to be extremely lucrative.

The Dark had been silently and secretly running the dark Web ever since its inception.

Over the years, as he'd ascended within the ranks of The Dark, he'd kept his activities hidden from his boss Alexei Vinokourov. He'd been his right-hand man for years, but Alexei had always thought he was dim-witted. Just how he'd wanted things to appear.

It had been worthwhile for him to act the fool for Alexei. But there had been too many times that he'd wanted to rip off the mask of stupidity and had nearly chewed through his tongue to keep from doing so.

His rise within The Dark had made all that groveling somewhat palatable. However, all that power came with responsibility and tonight he'd prove his devotion and allegiance to The Dark. He'd also reassert his dominance over the portion of The Dark that he controlled as director of the LA chapter.

His authority had been under attack lately, both overtly and covertly; tested and challenged by the men who served under him. They would like nothing better than to usurp his position and his rank.

Not going to happen. That shit would end tonight.

As he readied himself to log into the private virtual chat room, he thought back over the past few months of preparations.

He would clearly consecrate his position tonight with the sacrifice that he was presenting to the Supremacy and the Elders. But it was the video evidence that would reaffirm his devotion and his allegiance—and do it with flair.

He barely gave a passing thought to the role Marcus played in tonight's events; other than a brief reminiscence as to how this had all started a few months ago...

Marcus had become a liability, but after tonight he would no longer be a problem. The tipping point had been his ill-timed eavesdropping of privileged information about The Dark. He had unwittingly put the LA chapter, *my chapter*, of the Dark World in jeopardy.

And that would never do.

I would not tolerate anyone disrupting my operations no matter how integral they had proven to be. Most things in life came with an expiration date. A shelf life as it were. His would be dispatched sooner rather than later. Because in Marcus's case, what had once been integral was now obsolete.

I was in a back room at Club M where I had set up a makeshift office when I heard a knock at the door.

"Enter," I said, knowing full well it would be Marcus. I had texted Marcus to join me here for drinks and to discuss some business matters.

"Marcus," I said, as he stormed through the door clearly disgruntled.

"What's so urgent? I had plans with this hot little coed from USC. Tonight had better be worth my cancelled plans, Ivan," he said, emphasizing my name with a sneer.

"Why don't you pour us some drinks first. What I have planned for tonight will far surpass anything you could have planned or could have imagined. Believe me. I do hope you're *up* for an entertaining evening."

Marcus turned his head quickly at my statement. His eyes brightening with the anticipation and the promise inherent in my words. I had a feeling his excitement would diminish over the course of the evening.

"I'm always up and ready to go. No problems in that department." Marcus laughed at his juvenile sexual innuendo and cupped his balls for added emphasis; just in case I couldn't figure it out on my own.

"So what do you have planned for us later? Is there some new 'stock' that needs breaking in? Are we having another go at that little greeter, Lilly? I would love to tap that ass again."

I could see that Marcus was practically salivating at the prospect of fucking Lilly again.

"Liked her did you? Well I suspect she will be off for a few days recuperating from our very thorough attentions. I do plan to have her again. Though next time I won't be sharing her with you." I said with no small amount of disdain and despite my lack of subtlety, it still passed by Marcus unnoticed.

He handed me a tumbler of that rot gut whiskey he so favored, just as I knew he would. It didn't pay to be predictable and so he had no one to blame but himself for the outcome of tonight's activities. I set the glass down in front of me and watched as Marcus drained his glass in two quick swallows,then proceeded to fill his glass again. 'Bottoms up,' I thought.

I didn't actually have any business to discuss with Marcus, so I waited patiently for my evening plans to fall into place—which wouldn't take long at this rate.

I sent Yosef a quick text.

*We'll be there soon*

*Have the Luxe room ready*

"Let's get our evening started. Are you ready to go?"

Marcus stood up stumbling as he did so. "I sure am!" He stated overloud, "Yet's go! I mean...Let's go."

Two drinks and Marcus was already slurring his words.

Just perfect.

I grabbed his arm and we made our way down the musty corridor to the Luxe room. We were closed for the night, so all was quiet and my footsteps echoed crisply on the floor; whereas Marcus' footsteps were shuffling and obnoxious, grating on my last nerve.

Not for long.

# CHAPTER TEN

# Ivan

"Gentlemen, gentlemen," I said, as Marcus and I came through the door to the Luxe Room.

"I'm happy to see that you have all availed yourself of the bar. Thank you for coming to this special evening hosted by Club M, the Luxe room, and myself. I assure you that by the time you leave tonight, all your unique appetites will have been appeased and thoroughly sated."

I maneuvered Marcus to sit in one of the chairs and nodded to Yosef who brought me a drink and Marcus one as well. Drink in hand, I walked around the room conversing with the seven men who made up this private party.

I could see the gleam of wicked anticipation in each of their eyes. They all knew what was scheduled for the evening. The only one in the dark about the events for tonight was Marcus, though not for long.

"Marcus, do finish your drink. We are about to get started."

"Fantashtic!" He slurred, as he raised his glass up and with one quick flick of his wrist threw back the contents of his glass.

"Yet's get dis party shtarted. Damn it...I mean to shay...let's get this party started." He shook his head, as if that would make the words come as they should.

I watched as Marcus swayed in his seat and knew it was time.

"Gentlemen, why don't you step into the changing area and make yourselves more comfortable. I have taken the liberty to provide robes for you to wear. The entertainment will be ready in a few minutes." I watched as the seven men left the room; drinks in hand and joking with one another. Marcus stood up swaying on his feet, but ready to depart with the other men.

"No need to be shy, Marcus. You can change right here. Or perhaps you are too embarrassed about your inability to rise for the occasion? Hmmm? If that's the case, do feel free to stay dressed. You can watch the entertainment from over there," I said with obvious disdain, as I tipped my head towards the corner.

"Ha! As if! You know me better than that." Marcus said.

Marcus quickly shed his clothing. He pulled his shirt over his head and kicked off his shoes, not caring where they landed; an annoying habit he displayed on a regular basis. I laughed under my breath as he nearly fell over in his haste to get naked. No doubt the fear of sitting in the corner as a voyeur during the debauchery was goading his negligent disrobing.

He dropped his pants and gripped his cock in his right hand and began stroking himself, eyes on me with a look of triumph. I could hardly contain my need to wipe that smug look off his face and out of his eyes.

Patience.

"Having issues there, Marcus? Think you will be able to participate with that?" I asked with a raised eyebrow after giving his semi-hard cock a meaningful look. "If you can manage it, you've definitely earned the top spot for tonight."

"Oh, I can manage it."

I raised my right hand to my moustache, loving the textured feel of it under my thumb and forefinger while I stroked it and contemplated my next move.

Decision made.

I walked forward crowding in on Marcus. I was intentionally invading his space and maneuvering him in the direction that I wanted him to go. His mind was altered enough to move along the path I chose without challenging me. He was headed straight towards the waist-high padded table that had been secured to the floor.

Yosef walked in that direction too, but from the opposite side of the room and out of Marcus's field of vision. He would be there to assist me. Yosef had preemptively brought a few implements into the room that I might require for the evening, including that padded table that I was about to force Marcus to bend over.

"What. The. Fuck?" Marcus yelled.

I took my wing-tipped clad foot and kicked out at Marcus, sweeping his legs out from under him. I loved the sound of my shoe hitting his shins with a resonant *thunk*. As he lost his footing, I shoved him forcefully in the middle of his back. He hit the bench hard, landing on his chest with such force that it had knocked the breath right out of him. While he was gasping for breath

Yosef shoved a round bite block in and secured it tight behind his head.

I pulled his arms behind his back and bound them tight, but not at the wrist, as that would impair our access. So I zip-tied his right wrist to his left forearm and then repeated the process with his left wrist to his right forearm. Yosef quickly secured both of Marcus's legs so that they were widespread and fastened to the sturdy bench legs.

We finished at the same time. Marcus was caught and with no way to get free. Pre-planned and rapidly executed. I silently applauded myself and Yosef.

"Yosef, my drink if you will."

I walked slowly around Marcus and stopped at a point where I knew he could see me. Once I was assured that his attention was squarely on me and stayed there, I stopped walking and admired my work. I sipped at my drink and smiled. Everything had fallen quite nicely and literally into place.

Marcus was grunting and trying to tell me something, but that was made impossible with the way the bite block kept his jaw opened. No doubt he was spewing profanities at me. I smiled wider and sipped my drink again, licking my lips when a drop spilled over.

Marcus was foaming at that mouth. Drool was dripping down his chin. He looked much like a rabid dog that had been chained to a fence.

Yes, just like that.

But the fire that was leaping in his eyes and threatening me with retribution was laughable. I took the opportunity to do just that—and laughed in his helpless face.

One by one the seven men walked back into the Luxe room. They were wearing their masks and the silk robes I had provided for them; a superfluous affectation, as they wouldn't be wearing them for long. But the masks would remain to protect our identities during this special event.

The room was practically vibrating with sexual tension and felt alive with excitement. Layered over the buzzing anticipation was the heady scent of fear rolling off of Marcus in waves—much like the sweat that was rolling off his body to form little puddles under him. Both were an obvious testament to the fact that the drug-laced alcohol I had served him was wearing off.

Perfect—awake and aware just the way I liked them, but especially in Marcus's case.

"Now that we've reassembled we can finally get started. As promised, we have a special treat tonight and the star of our little show is none other than our good friend, Marcus. Please, cue the dramatic music if you would, Yosef."

I barked out a laugh at that, amused by my own wit. Though I wasn't entirely joking. I did want music playing in the background and Yosef started the selection that I had compiled just for tonight. I had put quite a bit of forethought into the atmosphere and mood I wanted to achieve for tonight's epic event.

Looking down at Marcus I could see awareness moving in his dark eyes. And it was that awareness—his realization of what was to come, that caused my instantaneous erection. I would make good use of it tonight, though not yet.

The seven men comprising the LA chapter of the Dark were very eager to get started, as they had been anticipating this evening for weeks now. They could use and abuse Marcus in whatever way they desired or could imagine—there were no restrictions. This was to be a special treat for these men.

A night of complete and utter debauchery.

A night about control.

I would watch the events unfold from behind the camera and then have the final turn of the night.

I deserved that and more.

And I planned to collect all that I was my due.

# CHAPTER ELEVEN

# Ivan

Marcus had been well and truly used. I enjoyed every minute of watching my men work him over. But, it was now my turn and I said as much. Though thoroughly sated, the men reluctantly retreated to the periphery of the room. They removed their masks as they settled well beyond the camera's voyeuristic eye.

I resentfully wore my full mask for the anonymity it provided while the camera was rolling. I hated the way the strings used to secure it messed with the perfection of my hair, but I had to concede defeat on that point.

Privacy trumped appearances, though not by much.

I strolled over to where Marcus could see me. Just as I had multiple times throughout the evening. I wanted to be sure that he knew I was still there and that I continued to document his humiliation and degradation.

He glared at me—the pain evident on his face and in the rigidness of his muscles. I smiled gleefully.

"Marcus, Marcus." I admonished. "You have only yourself to blame for your current predicament—bound and thoroughly used. You became too careless, too negligent of your duties, but above all—you were far too predictable and far too nosey. Now Marcus," I continued with the same condescending tone, "to make it in this business, in any business for that matter, one must never be too predictable. You see, predictability is the kiss of death—each and every time. The competition will eagerly capitalize on that. Just like I did tonight, and with a bit of panache, if I do say so myself."

I was more than just a little irritated with Marcus and getting more worked up by the moment. Now I would have to train someone new to take his place. Yosef was my right-hand-man and Marcus's job was well below his station and capabilities.

Trying to get these Millennials to self-motivate was virtually impossible. Lazy, the whole lot of them. I was fuming now. And my internal soliloquy spilled out, as I continued to walk circles around Marcus.

"The problem with the youth of today, those so called 'Millennials,'is that they think everything should be handed to them. They don't want to work for anything. They don't want to put forth any effort into succeeding. God forbid they pay some actual fucking dues. Or work up a sweat on their way to the top—where they might actually deserve to reap some rewards. Where's their fucking deserve-it factor?"

I removed my combat knife from its usual place on my belt. Then held it in a way Marcus was sure to see it.

"Where was yours, Marcus? You were greedy, Marcus. Too fucking greedy. But mostly you and your two friends were just—too—fucking—careless—and too fucking stupid—to live!"

I positioned myself behind Marcus. The sound of my zipper lowering caused Marcus to flinch.

With my knife was pressed against Marcus's rabbiting pulse, my gaze swept the room. I locked eyes with each and every one of my seven men. I let them see what I generally kept hidden.

But not tonight. No, not for this brief, but righteous moment.

I had a point to make, though this lesson would be lost on Marcus—but not on the other men in the room. Oh no, these men would learn this lesson and learn it well or pay a similar penalty.

"You know what Marcus, I'm not going to fuck you after all." I felt the rigidity of his muscles relax at my statement. "I deserve better than you. But you don't deserve anything, except this..."

My knife was quickly positioned so the spine was held tight in one hand and the handle in the other—like bookends to Marcus's neck.

I pulled my arms back. Hard and fast. And crushed Marcus's trachea. I had found over the years that the forefinger ring component of my combat knife was perfectly suited to aid in this maneuver. With deadly accuracy. Time and again. I stepped back and watched as he fought to breathe—and lost.

Struggling until he struggled no more.

I remained disappointed and dissatisfied. I hadn't been consumed by sated satisfaction, despite killing Marcus so gloriously.

I called out to one of the seven men. He sat smugly on the periphery of the room; engrossed in watching the events unfold. Especially the premature demise of Marcus.

There was another lesson yet to be delivered tonight.

*Don't get too big for your pants, or you'll find yourself without them—and on your knees putting your lying mouth to good use.*

The most vocal of my seven men was about to be delivered that very lesson and to my orgasmic satisfaction. Which could take a while, but I had nowhere else to be.

Yosef was already cleaning up the trash. So I would allow myself this well-deserved pleasure.

"Yosef, do not forget to deliver tonight's video to the people we discussed earlier. I'm sure they will be most interested in viewing tonight's *coup de grâce*." And I couldn't wait to present the clear evidence of my devotion to the Supremacy and the Elders in a few months at the virtual reaffirmation ceremony.

Assured that Yosef would fulfill all my desires and instructions in this matter, I returned my attention to the man kneeling before me. Staring down at him, I flicked my wrist, as if to say, "get on with it." I could see that this lesson would not be well received, but it would provide the necessary and desired impact. It would reverberate through the seven men gathered here tonight and my point would be well made.

Quinton Creighton might be the attorney of record for the LA division of our world, but he could be removed, as could any of these men. I didn't like his scheming ways in particular, so I had chosen him to be the lucky recipient of this lesson. I would enjoy reinforcing the fact that he was nothing and could be removed and replaced at my discretion.

While Quinton got busy working my cock, I looked over to Lilly Blue's father. He may have sacrificed his daughter to The Dark to gain entrance into our world, but he was part of the world that I controlled and I was angry with his missing daughter. I gave him a look that conveyed such. And by the look of fear on his face, he understood that he would be paying the price for her disobedience and soon.

My attention returned back to the man before me and my now flagging cock. I had let my anger with the disappearance of Lilly and Ava disrupt my reveling in this moment of power. When I met those two girls again—and I would meet them—they would pay the price for defying me.

# CHAPTER TWELVE

# Sage

I sent a text to Carter James to meet at his tattoo studio, L'Inked. He was like a brother to me and I trusted him implicitly. I would have met him at my home in Laurel Canyon, but I didn't want to take the chance that Ivan's goons would be watching for us to return there.

Meeting at Carter's place off of Melrose was an acceptable risk. It was highly unlikely that the goon squad would be watching Carter. However, I should've ditched the Stang somewhere and grabbed a different car. But it was too late to worry about that now. I'd just have a rental car delivered, I decided, as I parked in the alley behind the studio and reached for my cell.

Done. A nondescript sedan would be delivered within thirty minutes.

I walked around to Ava's door and opened it for her. I still hadn't decided where would be best place to take her. I couldn't bring myself to give control of her safety over to someone else.

We walked up to the backdoor of L'Inked. But erring on the side of caution, I had Ava stay in the alley next to the wall as I breached the door's threshold.

Looking to my right in the direction of the TV corner, I did a double take and stopped dead in my tracks. Sitting on the couch channel surfing was none-other-than Lilly Blue.

Fuck!

It had been months since I had seen her at Club M and what a difference they had made. She looked transformed—that was the only way I could describe her appearance.

I grabbed Ava's hand and we walked through the backdoor of L'Inked. Just as I was about to ask Lilly a few questions, Carter walked around the corner from the back.

He looked at Ava and me, and then over to Lilly. No words were needed. He walked over to where we stood and we embraced as the soul brothers that we were.

"Good to see you, Sage," Carter said as we broke away from each other and he stepped towards Ava. He extended his hand out to her and she shook it in greeting.

"Ava, good to see you again. You may not remember me, but I'm Carter James."

"So very nice to finally meet you. I wanted to thank you for helping to care for me that night a few months ago."

I heard footsteps just then and turned to see Lilly walk over to stand next to Carter. He pulled her protectively into his side as he placed his arm around her shoulders. I barely controlled my look of surprise, as I nodded my head to her and dove right in.

"Lilly, nice to see you again. This is my fiancée, Ava DeLaney. Ava, this is Lilly Blue."

Before either one of them could so much as say hello, Carter rudely interrupted,"Say what?" Carter said, as he tried to sound like an unbelieving asshat, but failed miserably. The huge congratulatory smile on his face was a dead giveaway.

"What can I say, I just knew it was right and that she was the right one. I'm very fortunate that Ava would consider taking a chance on me."

I watched as Carter looked down at Lilly. Strange that he hadn't mentioned her, not once in all of our conversations over the past several months and I was extremely curious as to why.

"Carter we need to talk," I looked at Lilly and Ava, then continued, "in private."

Ava took matters in hand.

"Lilly, can we go sit down for a bit?" Ava asked.

She didn't wait for an answer and started walking towards the couch located in the TV corner. Carter and I watched them go.

"First things first, I made a rookie mistake in driving the Stang over here. I phoned a car rental place and they will be dropping off a car in thirty. Can I keep the Stang in your storage unit?"

"Of course. No problem at all. So what's going on? You said you'd fill me in when you got here. You're here, so tell me."

I nodded my head over towards the corner where Lilly and Ava were talking.

"Let's talk about you and Lilly first. I distinctly remember asking you to go get her, but I don't remember asking you to keep her." I gave him a pointed look that got my message across and waited for his response. But by the look on his face I had a feeling I'd be waiting until hell froze over.

"What's going on, Sage?"

"Like that is it?" I laughed out loud, pulling Lilly and Ava's attention in our direction. I had a feeling that I wouldn't be getting much information from Carter, but that was okay. All in due time. He'd spill eventually.

"I can't tell you much. I have some unfinished business to take care of. And I will have to go this alone because there are sensitive things from the past that need investigating. What I can say is that I may be off-line for a while. I may have to take Ava to her father's eventually, but I'm not willing to do so yet."

"Man, that grates. I know you won't be happy about that eventuality. Not at all. I wouldn't be either." He looked towards Lilly before continuing, "The need to protect her yourself would make that difficult, if not impossible to swallow."

"Yeah, I can't say I'm exactly happy about it, far from it. But I do know that Alexei will protect her with his life if need be."

"So how can I help?"

"Hiding my car in your storage unit will be a huge help. But after seeing Lilly, I have a feeling you might be able to help me in a way that I hadn't expected. What can you tell me about Ivan? When you went to retrieve Lilly at Club M all those months ago, did you happen to hear anything? Pick up any info?" I knew it was a long shot, but I had to ask even though the information would be old by now.

"There's not much I can tell you. The bouncer at the entrance to Club M was a right douche bag and was determined not to let me in. I had to do some name drop-ping just to get through the door. The staff, whether by choice or not, were drugged and not much help. The club members, as you can well imagine, were not forth-coming with any information. I was lucky to have found Lilly sitting outside next to a foul smelling dumpster."

"Why in the world was she sitting outside next to a stinking dumpster? When I left her she was inside re-cuperating from the scene we did on stage."

"I *do not* want to hear about your scene with my Lil-ly," Carter said, in a tone of voice I had never heard from him before. "She was recuperating all right, but not from your scene. I still don't know what happened after you left her there. She won't tell me. And I won't press her for the details. But some fucking sadist drugged her, then used and abused her, going so far as to dislocate her shoulder in the process. And that's how I found her, cradling her arm and in a tremendous amount of pain."

# CHAPTER THIRTEEN

# Lilly

## Club M—Months Prior

I needed to stand up and I would in a minute, if I could manage it. I was beyond exhausted at this point and not certain that my legs would support me. I could not exactly recall how I managed to make it outside. But now that I was aware of my surroundings I realized I was sitting on the ground and leaning against the brick wall next to where the huge dumpster was located. Perhaps I thought this would be a less than obvious hiding place, because who in their right mind would sit down next to *that* stench on purpose.

The more aware I became, the more pain I seemed to be in. The asphalt was rough under my butt and my thighs. However, the sharp digging rocks paled in comparison to the blow torch that was my vagina and rectum; courtesy of Ivan the Impaler. Though I knew he must have had help in that regard.

Ivan was my sadistic Russian *boss*. He operated some of the sex clubs in and around LA, like Club M. He had not been happy about the scene I had participated in with Sage. Ivan wanted to be sure that I knew, as well as felt, his displeasure and had set out to erase all the beautiful sensations that I had been feeling.

God forbid I had a moment of respite away from the greeting position he continually placed me in or a moment of pleasure for myself. He rarely drugged me over the past couple of years, but tonight he injected something into my veins as an additional punishment.

I had lost some, but not all of what had been done to me in that back room. I could not decide which was worse. Knowing or not. In Ivan's deranged mind, that scene with Sage had been all my fault. Therefore, I needed to pay the consequences for allowing someone else to touch me.

As if I could have said no.

In all honesty I probably would have volunteered if only to get out of greeting for just a little while. I was beyond tired of having random men shove their cocks into my mouth with my arms tied behind my back. Forced to wear that heinous slave collar while balancing precariously on my spread knees.

Had I known how Sage would treat me on that stage —I would have begged to do that scene. Never in my life had I been made to feel like that. I may no longer be a virgin, but I had never received pleasure before—quite the opposite in fact.

Therefore, I could not even properly articulate the words to describe the feelings that scene had invoked— not even within the safe confines of my own head. I would break it all down later. Try to figure it all out. Or maybe I would just leave it be. Perhaps there was no need to analyze it beyond the beautiful moment that it was.

I looked at my right shoulder to see why it was hurting...

That had been a mistake. Waves of nausea overtook me and I started salivating with the need to vomit. The joint was grossly deformed and I had to quickly avert my eyes. I started retching which jostled my shoulder causing more pain and more waves of nausea. So I supported my arm by gently cradling it across my chest.

I feared that my shoulder had been dislocated or worse. Compliments of Ivan, I am sure.

Sadist!

I had a vague recollection dancing through my head of Ivan twisting my right arm up and behind my back. Pushing the limits of its flexibility without a care.

Now that I was aware of my injury, the throbbing pain increased exponentially and quickly eclipsed the burning pain resonating from below.

Tears leaked out from behind my closed lids as I tried to gather the will to stand up and go home. Getting away from Ivan permanently was not an option, but at least I could go home and get cleaned up. I needed a bath consisting of hot water, bleach, soap, and no doubt an antibiotic. Not that I had access to any. But considering I was not able to stand yet, I would settle for a drink of water.

I sighed to myself.

Where was this James Something-or-other? The guy Sage was supposedly sending to my rescue. I am sure he must have left when he could not find me.

"By all that's holy! Please tell me that you are the ever elusive Lilly Blue," said a gruff voice on the other side of my closed eyes.

I flinched at the unexpected intrusion and gave a grunt of pain. Ah, the tatted and pierced James had finally come to the rescue. Or rather I assumed that was who was talking to me.

I could only wish that he would have come earlier—before the back room bingo had started. There was a sudden brightness behind my closed lids, like a light shining upon my face.

"Yes, I am Lilly Blue. Are you James?"

"Carter."

"Carter? I thought it was James."

"Carter James."

"You are confusing me. Is it James or Carter?"

"Lilly Blue?"

"Yes."

"Will you please open your eyes and look at me for a moment?" He asked.

I did as he requested and opened my eyes, but gasped as I did so. He had squatted down and was directly in front of me, instead of hovering over me.

"Hi, Lilly Blue. Let me clear up this confusion. My first name is Carter and my last name is James. Sage said you needed a ride home. Have you changed your mind? I've been searching for hours trying to find you."

"Well, first name Carter and last name James, I told Sage that if you ever showed up, I would decide then as to whether or not I would go with you."

"I've shown up, Miss Lilly. Will you come with me?"

That was the question of the hour.

"I have to be honest. I had no intention of going with you. But now I might have to. Or at least I might need your help with standing."

I hated asking for help. "Would you please help me to stand?" I asked with quiet desperation.

His steady gaze was comforting, yet disconcerting at the same time. I wanted to see the color of his eyes, but it was impossible to see with the way everything had been cast in shadows. He adjusted his squatting position and a stray bit of light reflected off the piercing in his bottom lip.

It was only for a brief moment because a split second later, his lip and the piercing disappeared into his mouth. He sucked on it and worried it with his teeth before he taking a breath to speak.

"What happened to your shoulder?"

I did not answer him. I could not make myself say the words. How could I admit that what had happened to me was in essence all my fault—due to my inaction.

Complacency was the devil in disguise.

He let loose of his glistening lip and shook his head. I am sure realizing it was futile. I was not going to answer him.

"Let me see what I can do. May I touch your shoulder?"

He dropped to his knees before me, heedless of the rough pavement digging into the skin of his kneecaps. With his hands resting patiently on his thighs and his head slightly bowed, he waited for me to answer.

I had to turn my face away from the arresting vision that was Carter. "Yes, Carter, you may touch me."

I felt his fingers skim lightly across the deformity of my swollen shoulder. He brushed aside the black t-shirt Sage had given me to wear—fully exposing the injury.

I heard his rapid intake of breath and despite myself looked back at my shoulder. I quickly averted my eyes again, but not before I saw the dark bruising that covered the pale skin of my shoulder. I focused on the brick wall across from me and took slow, deep breaths to manage the nausea.

"Let's get you onto your feet and see what I can do."

He stood up first, then bent over to assist me with standing. He was very gentle. I barely had to help in the process of getting me upright and onto my feet.

It still took my breath away. I was swaying on my feet due to the pain from my shoulder and the aching bits that shall remain nameless.

Carter kept a firm hold on me, presumably to keep me from falling over.

Then quick as a snake and before I had time to react, Carter had managed to put my shoulder back into place. I thought he was reaching out to steady me when he had cupped my right elbow. But before I had time to say, *thank you*, he had lifted my elbow up and back—guiding the joint back into its proper place.

At first I had tilted my head back and smiled a dopey, yet grateful smile up at Carter. I thought him quite clever for being all stealthy-like and not warning me before it manipulated my shoulder. But that was before the pain hit me like a sledgehammer.

Between one breath and the next—I was out.

# CHAPTER FOURTEEN

# Carter

I could have stared into Lilly's eyes for hours getting lost in their shifting color,but she was clearly in considerable pain. So I reluctantly checked the impulse to do so.

I had the feeling I needed to get her out of that alley and away from Club M quickly. After getting her upright, I decided to put her shoulder back into place without warning her first. I had adjusted my brother Erich's shoulder multiple times over the years while growing up and was confident I knew what to do.

I felt horrible for hurting Lilly, but had found through trial and error that putting the shoulder back into place quickly had always worked best. However, I'll never forget the look on her face just before the pain had overwhelmed her. At first I felt the hero to her heroine, but now I felt very much the villain. Nothing to be done for it. I'd have to apologize to her when she came 'round.

As I made my way to the car, I barely registered her weight as I carried her out of the alley. She was like a petite pixie waif, especially with her pale skin, short black hair, and jewel-toned eyes. She had an aura of a misty forest about her. The artist in me wanted to draw her in what was clearly her natural habitat—the land of the faeries from which she had been abducted. Or at least that was what my fanciful mind envisioned for her.

Sage was right about her. She was indeed unique.

I had been hanging out at my tattoo studio, L'Inked, when Sage called me. He asked for me to come and rescue Lilly. He hadn't necessarily put it so boldly, but that's what it was—a rescue.

As a detective working undercover, he often trolled through the dregs of society and would call me out of the blue to come pick someone up that was in need of help. I was the only one that knew the truth about who Sage really was. We felt it would be safer for Sage and everyone else involved, so we kept that a secret between us.

Before finding Lilly outside by that rank smelling dumpster, I had spent a couple of hours searching through Club M for her. Naturally, no one inside the club would point her out to me or even admit that she had ever been there. Besides, all of the working staff appeared to have been drugged, so it was doubtful they cared about where Lilly might be. And the fucked-up, sadistic club members were a complete and total bust.

So here I was, hours later, carrying my abused pixie away to safety. Retribution was coursing through my blood and indecision nagging at my mind. I couldn't decide where to take Lilly. Instinct or a sixth sense of sorts, was pushing me to take her to my place and considering I had no idea where she lived, that was the most viable option.

But as we approached my 1972 blue and white Ford Gran Torino, Lilly stirred in my arms and opened her eyes to look up at me. The pain was evident, but she barely acknowledged its hold.

"Ouch," she said with a furrowed brow.

She turned her face towards my chest and leaned her head against it. No doubt attempting to hide her pain from me. I would let her escape my gaze for now, but that would change.

"Lilly, I don't know anything about your situation and I won't pry, but I think you should come to my place to recuperate. After you're feeling better we can figure out what to do. But I think it would be best for you, if you could heal without having to worry over whether or not someone would be coming after you. How does that sound?"

"I do not wish to be a bother."

I had to strain to hear her words because like a reluctant confession they had barely slipped out of her mouth and were almost lost to the wind. I didn't know much about Lilly yet, but what I did know was that my pixie didn't like to ask for help. I wondered why—pride or lessons harshly learned?

I had a sinking suspicion the later was the culprit. Thankfully, it felt like she had a bit of pride and spunkiness left, though barely enough to keep her going despite life's adversities.

"It's no bother at all. Actually, I insist, as I need to get home to my Missy. She will no doubt be wondering where I've been all night and be missing me." I felt Lilly stiffen slightly in my arms.

"You must be in tremendous pain. When we get to my place, I'll give you some pain medicine. Not too much, but enough to take the edge off so that you can rest."

Once at my Torino, I placed Lilly gently onto her feet. I unlocked and opened the passenger door. It was fortunate that her right shoulder was injured and not her left. I would be able to maneuver her into the car with the least amount of pain.

Reaching across her, I grabbed the lap belt and secured it. And for once, I appreciated the fact that this particular car lacked a shoulder strap.

When I was settled into my seat and likewise belted in, I turned to Lilly and gave her an assessing once-over. The soft light loved her face and I was captivated. It also highlighted the fact that she was exhausted and fading fast.

"Why don't you lean your head back and rest if you can. I don't live too far away—just over in Silver Lake. It shouldn't take us long to get home; especially at this time of the morning." She nodded and acquiesced, leaning her head back.

"When we arrive home I'll introduce you to Missy. I'm sure you guys will get along well. We've been together for about four years now and honestly I couldn't be happier. She came into my life at a time when—well let's just say, she saved me from myself."

"It just figures." I thought I heard her mumble, but I hesitated to ask her.

Instead, I turned on the radio to something soothing. I was hoping it would help her to relax, as I drove us home and into the coming dawn.

# CHAPTER FIFTEEN

# Lilly

I must have fallen asleep on the way to Carter's home in Silver Lake. But I came awake when I felt the Torino roll to a stop. I turned my head so I could look over at Carter.

He was nibbling on his piercing again and scraping his teeth across his bottom lip. I could hear the metal labret occasionally hit his teeth. I could not look away. I was mesmerized by how his plump bottom lip kept popping out from between his teeth—fuller and moistened by the repeated action.

I quickly turned my head away. It seemed pointless to look when I would be meeting, "Missy" in just a few moments.

"I must have fallen right to sleep," I said after turning my head back to look out the front windshield.

"Yeah, pretty much. The minute the wheels started to roll forward, you were out and snoring," he said, with a chuckle under his breath.

"I beg your pardon, I do not snore," I said with a sniff of mortification, because maybe I had been snoring. I was beyond exhausted.

He laughed at the face I made and I laughed with him.

"Come on. Let's get you inside, cleaned up, and fed so that you can have some pain medicine and get some sleep. I plan to give you some ibuprofen, because I think you may have been drugged at some point tonight. We shouldn't take any chances with combining medications." Carter said with a note of concern in his voice.

I did not want to admit it to him that he was right in his assumptions, but at this point he deserved at least a fraction of the truth. Or a part of the truth that I was willing to share.

"You are right. I was injected with something tonight—to keep me compliant. So there are portions of the night that I can only vaguely recall...and I am okay with that," I said as my voice trailed off at the end. I had no desire to fill in those gaps.

I turned back to Carter. By the way he was looking at me with his chocolate-brown eyes, he must have heard what I had mumbled under my breath. The muscles of his jaw tightened before he turned his gaze away from me to look out the front windshield.

After a deep,controlled exhale, he hopped out the car and came to my side. I sensed that he was upset. I was not sure as to the cause, but I assumed it was me. I had kept him out and awake all night.

He helped me out of the car with ease. And thankfully, now that my shoulder had been reset, it was not as painful as I had expected.

"Thank you." I said, as I reached out with my left hand and placed it gently on his colorfully inked arm.

The warmth of his skin was shocking to my cold hand, as if the colorfully inked flames provided heat in truth. I wanted to leave my hand there for the warmth he provided, but I knew I had to pull it away and I did so reluctantly.

Since I was still standing next to him, he placed his right hand on my lower back to offer his support as we made our way to the front door.

"I know you must be in pain and clearly you're exhausted. Once you've met Missy, I'll show you where the bathroom is. Then you can take a shower and get cleaned up. I'll make you some scrambled eggs and toast that way you don't have to take the ibuprofen on an upset stomach. Or that's what my Mom always told me," he said with obvious affection.

His thoughtfulness and simple act of caring were so outside my realm of experience that I was not sure how to act or reply. So I kept it brief, but heartfelt and said, "Thank you, Carter." I tried to keep the emotion out of my voice, but I was fairly certain it had colored those three words in bright neon.

He unlocked and opened the front door but instead of letting me precede him through the doorway, he went in first. I rolled my eyes in my head thinking to myself, well that was not very mannerly, but completely normal in my world. Though it did almost appear as if he were trying to protect me, but from what I could not be certain. The only person he had mentioned was Missy and that was whom I was expecting to meet.

I had just stepped through the doorway when I heard a noise off to my right. And for the life of me, I could not figure out what it could be. But whatever the noise was, it was growing louder. Just then, barreling around the corner came the biggest dog I had ever seen in my life. I am not ashamed to admit that I stepped back—by several feet.

"Missy! Stop. Sit," Carter said with an authoritative tone that was accompanied by a quick snap of his fingers and a point to the floor. The huge grey dog sat immediately.

I felt the need to respond to his tone as well, but refrained—barely.

"This is the Missy you wanted me to meet? A Great Dane?" I could not keep the incredulous tone from my voice.

"Yes, this is my Missy."

I smiled beatifically.The affection that he had for Missy was apparent to see. But, if I had known Carter well enough, I would have smacked him on the back of the head for leading me to believe that Missy was his girlfriend. A little bubble of happiness floated through me, but I would not be examining the source of that. Nope, I chose to ignore it instead.

Uncertain of what Missy might think of me, I decided to stay right where I was—tucked behind Carter's back. However, I did peek around his shoulder to check out his beautiful dog. She was gazing at her master in adoration. I was struck by the oddity of her big, beautiful eyes.

Carter turned around to see what I was doing and laughed when he saw I was tucked behind him, but peeking around his shoulder. He turned so he was sideways to myself and Missy, but giving me a better view of her. Grabbing my left hand with his right, we walked forward to greet Missy properly.

The closer we came to the grey dog, the more I could see what an absolute love she was. Her big bi-colored eyes were shining with intelligence and watching me with an inquisitive, yet guarding nature. I had always wanted a dog of my own, but the nature of my life had made that an impossibility.

"Lilly Blue, may I present to you, Missy, the love of my life."

Carter turned to smile at me. I could see that his words were true—she was in fact the love of his life. I tried to pull my hand away from his so that I could pet Missy. But as I tried to pull my hand away he stayed me with his words.

"She is very protective of me, Lilly, so keep your hand in mine and I will introduce your hand for her to smell. That way she will know that you mean me no harm and will relax her guard," Carter told me.

As he was telling me this, I was nodding my head in understanding. I did not really understand, but it made sense. Besides which, Missy was a big dog and I would not be surprised if she were taller than me when standing on her back legs. Heck, I was barely taller than her now and she was sitting. Oh, the joys of being so tiny and vertically challenged.

With our hands still joined, Carter placed them directly in front of Missy and under her nose. With a nod from Carter, she nudged our joined hands and gave me a welcoming lick. I am certain I did not smell the best and felt fortunate to have received her warm welcome and not a nibble on my hand.

Thankfully, she had not caught a whiff of Ivan's unique stench coating my skin. She would have attacked for sure. I would have, or rather I would have liked to, not that it would have changed the outcome in any way.

I could feel the helplessness overtaking me again, but Carter pulled me from my dark thoughts before they spiraled out of control.

"Now that the introductions have been made, I won't have to worry about Missy making a chew toy out of my little pixie," he laughed at that, "Let me show you where you can get cleaned up. And I'll start some breakfast."

His house seemed like the typical male abode: black comfy couch in an open-concept family room, the requisite TV, and a minimalist approach to furniture. But the soft white walls were another thing altogether.

Everywhere that I looked was an explosion of color. Artwork in various mediums were displayed about the room and I was drawn towards them. I felt more awake now after seeing all the vibrant colors expressed within the beautiful artwork.

I walked around the room, lost in thought, as I absorbed the beauty before me. I loved to doodle, not that anyone knew about that. But this—this was so beyond my amateur scribbles. I looked at Carter, then back to the art. I was drawn to each of them for the emotions that they evoked.

"These are incredible."

I did not know how to describe what I saw before me or how they made me feel. And at the fear of sounding completely ignorant, I stopped with that one statement and continued to walk about the room absorbing all that I saw.

I loved the varied colors that were present and showcased. The plain walls were a perfect backdrop. Some were loud and vibrant, announcing to the world in no uncertain terms to look at them. While others were subtle and subdued, but captured my attention just as avidly for what they whispered, instead of what they screamed.

"Are these yours?"

"Yes, they're mine."

The quiet way he answered that question didn't lend itself to further inquiry, but I was too curious about something Sage had said. So before I could stop myself I blurted out my question, though it was not the one I had really wanted to ask.

"Sage said that you were not involved in the club scene. So what do you do, Carter? Are you an artist?

"I am, though not in a traditional sort of way. I use skin as my canvas."

"What do you mean by that—tattoos?"

"Yes, I own a place off Melrose called, L'Inked Tattoo Studio."

I searched his face and his eyes before I dropped my gaze to travel over his inked skin. His tattoos were as vibrant and as beautiful as the artwork on the walls. I wondered if he had inked his own skin as well and asked him so.

"Yes, I did some of the ink on my skin, but not all of it. I'm very right-hand dominant, so a fellow artist did the tattoos on my right arm and all the places I couldn't reach."

Carter ended his statement with a slight raising of his dark eyebrow, which I took to mean there might be some places with ink that were not up for discussion. I shook my head to myself. I would not be asking where those places might be. Of course, now my imagination was running wild and I could not stop thinking about where.

"Thank you for humoring me and allowing me the time to look at your artwork. It truly is exceptional."

"You're welcome. Now, follow me and I'll take you to the bathroom."

"Lead the way. I am most definitely ready to clean the filth off of me." I probably should have kept that last statement to myself, but it snuck out before I could censor myself.

Carter stopped and looked down at me. "Lilly, will you tell me what happened tonight before I arrived? I know that you had met Sage earlier in the evening because he had called and told me to come and get you. But what happened after he left?"

I wanted to answer, I really did, but instead I looked up at him—mute with shame and shook my head. I hated to disappoint him, but I just could not utter the words.

Tears clogged my throat, so I had to clear it several times and loudly swallowed just to say, "Thank you for your concern,but I must keep this to myself. I hope that you understand." I dropped my gaze to the floor, not wanting to see his disappointment.

Carter reached out his hand to tip my chin up—gently forcing me to raise my eyes to his. He had moved his right hand from my chin to the side of my face and cradled my cheek. With the pad of his thumb he gently wiped away the tear that slid silently from the corner of my eye. I felt the warm metal from his tungsten thumb ring slide across my cheek as well.

"It's okay. I shouldn't have asked. Just know that if you want to talk, I'll be here to listen. And without judgement."

"Okay. Thank you."

I showered and wished with all my heart that I could cleanse my soul as easily as my skin. I feared those stains would remain, making me forever tainted.

Plus, the sins of my father—those marked me through and there would be no escape from them.

So it was pointless to think or to dream about what might have been—in a normal world.

Move on, Lilly, he is so above your grasp.

# CHAPTER SIXTEEN

# Sage

"After hearing that story, I can see why you've kept Lilly with you. I'm sure Ivan was involved and I wouldn't doubt that he's been looking for her ever since she disappeared. Keep that in mind," I said.

Carter explained how he found Lilly outside of Club M sitting by a dumpster. I should have never left her there. Her mistreatment could be laid at my feet.

That sin would be added to the collection of others that indelibly marked my soul.

"He can't have her back!" Carter said, with the vehemence I rarely heard from him, but completely understood.

"So here's what you can do for me. I need to use your computer. I know that you're a closet techie," I teased him. "Your store computer probably has some safe-guards that my computer wouldn't have. I can't use any of the computers at the precinct without raising questions. As far as they know, I'm still hiding in the mountains with Ava. I want to keep it that way for now."

"Sure thing. Go use the one in my office. It's more secure than the employee one at the counter. Just shut the door so you can have some privacy." He directed me before walking over to sit next to Lilly and Ava.

Once in the office I did as Carter directed and shut the door. The computer was already up and running. I walked over and woke it up by moving the mouse. I was a little surprised that Carter hadn't instituted some type of passcode to access the computer, but Carter was confident that none his employees would mess with his private computer. Besides they were all like one big family.

I plugged the jump drive into the USB port and waited for the computer to recognize it. A moment later and dead center on the screen was a folder named, The Dark.

I moved the cursor to hover over the folder and clicked to open it. I was prompted to enter the security code that Tomi had mentioned in her letter. I typed in the day, the month, and the year that Tomi and I had gone to the Griffith Observatory.

I had no idea what to expect, but at minimum I thought I would find some the information that Tomi had alluded to. But what I found were instructions on how to access something called the deep web.

What the hell!

The instructions directed me on how to open something called a Tor encryption browser. Whatever that was. And once that opened, I was to enter the URL address provided in the folder. This address would take me to the information I needed. I sat there at a loss. I wasn't sure what I should do.

Was Carter's computer private enough that I could proceed without detection? I needed to ask him, yet I didn't want to involve him too deeply in whatever danger this could present. There were already numerous deaths associated with this information. I wouldn't put Carter, Lilly, or Ava in more danger. Not if I could help it.

Deciding to ask, rather than assume, I stepped to the office door and motioned for Carter. He walked over and I asked him about the security of his computer and the possibility for detection and tracking. He told me I should be fine. He went on to discuss how he knew all was safe, but he lost me at bouncing IP addresses.

The more I learned about this case, the less I knew. What in the world had Tomi uncovered with the help of her husband?

I followed the directions contained within that Dark folder. And in doing so, I started a chain reaction of events that led me straight into the dark and a deadly web of intrigue that I could have neither predicted, nor prepared for.

# CHAPTER SEVENTEEN

# Scar

It was *go* time.

She put her phone away after reading the notification that had flashed across her screen. She hadn't expected the heralded message to be delivered today—if ever—popping up like a ghost from the ever-present past, jarring and unexpected.

After all this time, why couldn't it have just stayed lost and forgotten? Now she would have to alter her plans—years in the making—and accelerate her end game.

Time had started and she could feel it counting down.

She piled her long red hair on top of her head and placed her sunglasses onto her crooked nose. Grabbing her belongings, she walked out of the pay-by-the-hour motel room. She astutely avoided the mirror as she closed the door behind her.

Stepping out into the bright LA sunshine, she took in a deep breath to rid her lungs and nasal passages of the stench clinging to them.

It had been a long time since she had been to the City of Angels. Not much had changed—just her.

She was only here on business and had no desire to reconnect with any of her old friends. Not that they would have recognized her in any case. Or visited this part of LA—definitely not her former stomping grounds.

As she walked to the car, she congratulated herself for remembering the events of the night before. Whether she wanted to remember them or not was another matter altogether.

She looked back over her shoulder to see if anyone was behind her.

All clear.

She would have pitied the person following in her wake. For today, she was sporting a heavy dose of that new *en vogue* perfume. She just *knew* it would give Chanel a run for its money.

*Eau de Stale Smoke and Mildew*! It was sure to go viral.

Right!

She would have to add that lovely stench to whatever else was clinging to her unwashed skin, making her a trifecta of fucked-up. Sighing, Scar shook her head and thought...

How far she'd fallen.

# CHAPTER EIGHTEEN

# Sage

Following the directions in the Dark folder, I accessed the deep web through the Tor encryption browser. Then launched the given URL address. I had no idea what I was doing—a rare and uncomfortable sensation.

Five minutes ago I knew nothing about the deep web. And five minutes later—I still didn't.

But the one thing I did know with an absolute certainty was that Brent Delacourt was a complete and utter asshole.

The hair on the back of my neck had rose in alarm when I saw there was a file within the Dark folder with my name on it. I clicked to open it and began reading. And that's when I knew that without a doubt that he was a narcissistic prick.

Mother-fucking-son-of-a-bitch!

If Brent weren't already dead, I think I would have killed him myself! Though perhaps not in the same fashion. Brent's death had been particularly gruesome and hardcore. But I understood the viciousness of it now.

Over five years ago, Tomi had come home to find that the three men charged with guarding her family were dead, murdered by Alexei it was presumed at the time. And according to the CSI reports, when Tomi entered the front door of her home, she had been greeted by the sight of her husband Brent—hanging from the bannister in the foyer.

Dead and brutally eviscerated.

Her daughter Emma had been upstairs in her bedroom—murdered and laying in her toddler bed. For that alone, I would stop at nothing to solve this mystery for Tomi and find justice for her daughter.

Before disappearing, Tomi had reached out to my grandfather Pete. When I returned home for his funeral, I had found a note from Tomi in his desk. The note mentioned a package she wanted me to look after, but I had never found it. And my attempts to investigate what happened to Tomi and that package had led to nowhere.

I returned to my undercover assignment frustrated and grieving. Because not only had my grandfather died unexpectedly, but Tomi had gone missing along with whatever she had wanted to tell me.

Until now, that is. Ava found it buried in one of those boxes at the cabin. But why my grandfather would hide the package there was just another mystery to be solved.

I hoped to find detailed information in these files that would lead me towards finding justice for Tomi. Instead, what I had found were more questions and a mounting hatred for Tomi's husband.

*Sage, I'm sure you're wondering what the hell is going on. As you probably know by now, Tomi led the investigation into Alexei Vinokourov's black market activities.*

*But Tomi had no idea what was really going on with Alexei and neither did the LAPD.*

*Shortly after they started their investigation, I started one of my own. Thinking to help Tomi. But an unexpected secret surfaced. One that had been buried deep and shouldn't have been discovered.*

*But I'm just that good.*

*I needed time to decide what to do with this new information and created a diversion for Tomi and the LAPD while I did so.*

*It's what I eventually did with the information that led you and me, to this place and time.*

*Read the file marked Alexei. In there you will have the misinformation that I fed to Tomi. She trusted me and the information that I showed her.*

*That was a mistake on her part because Alexei was one of the good guys. Go figure. But his wasn't the juicy secret that I'd uncovered.*

*By the way, this folder can only be accessed by you, Tomi, and myself. However, only you and I will know the true contents of these files.*

*Tomi thought she knew everything, but she didn't.*

*I changed what was in the Dark folder after she initially read it. I couldn't allow her to discover the true depth and scope of where her investigation was heading. So I did whatever I could to lead Tomi away from the truth that she sought.*

*The other files in the Dark folder are my insurance. Should I die, by either natural causes or by the hands of another, these files will act as my tell-all. As my backup plan.*

*You, Sage, are my backup plan.*

*Surprise, mother-fucker.*

*I want vengeance and I will use you to obtain it.*

*And you'll do it too because you are a truth seeker—just like Tomi.*

*Though I know you'll want to walk away, I know that you won't. You'll stop at nothing to help Tomi and I'll use that to control you.*

*If you're reading this file and this message, then I'm already dead.*

*But if I'm dead, then Tomi can finally have what she has always wanted—You.*

*Despite being away and undercover for most of my marriage to Tomi, you were always there between us. A barrier that prevented us from reaching true intimacy. I even questioned the paternity of my own daughter because of you!*

It was disconcerting to have a one-sided conversation with a dead man. I found myself wanting to fire questions at him or yell profanities at the computer—as if he could hear me.

*I don't know how much time has passed since my death, but the steps you will be taking and the information that you will be acquiring should be timeless. All of this will eventually lead you to the answers that you need.*

*It will point you towards this secret society I discovered by accident and eventually you'll discover the man behind the proverbial curtain. And he's the one that you'll ulti-mately want to find.*

*Evil that one. Pure unadulterated evil!*

*I'm sure you have a million questions, yet have no idea what to ask or where to start.*

*But you will, after...*

What in the hell had Brent involved himself in? Did he realize that he had put his daughter and his wife in jeopardy for whatever he had discovered or was involved in? If he were here and alive, I would beat the hell out of him. I would get all the information that I needed from him—after I had vented my anger.

Instead, I would be doing this cloak and dagger bullshit and chasing my tail, jumping through the hoops that he had designed just to fuck with me. I disliked his arrogant ass to begin with, but this crap had only solidified it.

Reading back through what little information Brent had actually provided, I didn't have much to go on. I obviously couldn't trust any of the information at face value, yet I would have to pursue whatever leads he provided.

Brent was correct in that I didn't know what questions to ask, not yet that is. One thing was for certain though, whoever or whatever Brent was involved with had definitely pointed the investigators towards Alexei.

Brent stated that Alexei was nothing more than a figurehead or a scapegoat for the criminal activities that Tomi and the LAPD had been investigating.

Could this secret society Brent was referring to actually know the true purpose of Alexei's position?

Could they have known that Alexei had been deep undercover working for the FBI for more than 20 years? That would definitely put an interesting spin on things, but I wouldn't think so, otherwise they would have chosen a different fall guy.

It felt as if I knew less now than I did when opening the file. I was confused and that was definitely not a place where I was comfortable. I didn't like having someone else in control. Brent knew me too well in that regard.

I wanted to ask the questions and quickly find the answers—not have them handed out to me piecemeal by a man who was annoyingly cryptic. And who had a need to be vindictive from the grave.

*You will eventually acquire the information that I died for. Information that you need to exact my revenge.*

*Are you ready, Sage?*

*Welcome to the Dark!*

*May it drag you down and swallow you whole.*

# CHAPTER NINETEEN

# Ava

On our drive to LA, we hadn't discussed where we were going. So I was completely taken by surprise when we stopped by the tattoo studio where I had first met Sage. It was a welcomed, yet unexpected detour. But it gave me the opportunity to thank Carter for his help when I stumbled into his studio that night—looking like a crack whore to be sure.

Carter was an attractive guy with chocolate-brown eyes and messy brown hair that was threaded with auburn. He had colorful tattoos and several piercings. Not what I was usually attracted to.

But the way his lip piercing accentuated the plumpness of his bottom lip—yup, I could totally see the attraction of that. It kind of made me want to take a bite out of it. I felt myself flush a bit and knew my stupid pale skin would be glowing.

I glanced at Sage. His only response was a raised eyebrow. I shook my head. I wasn't going to explain my thoughts.

I met Lilly and I have to admit that it was a little awkward at first. But I had her at a distinct disadvantage. I knew who she was and what had occurred be-tween her and Sage—while she didn't know who I was.

I tried not to let any of that color my view of her or our conversation,and I don't think that it did.

She was such a sweet little thing. Not at all what I expected. Though I didn't really know what I expected.

She reminded me of a subdued version of Willow. Both girls were petite and incredibly beautiful, though Lilly's was more of a quiet beauty and Willow's was more flamboyant—a nod to her red hair and fiery tem-per.

We didn't ask each other too many questions,but from what I gathered, she had been with Carter the whole time that Sage and I had been away and in the mountains. Lilly and Carter seemed to be together as a couple, but that was just a guess on my part.

Their body language suggested as much.

We left the Stang with Carter and took off once our rental car arrived. Sage seemed frustrated and on edge after reading whatever had been on that flash drive. I asked him about it, but he felt that it would be safer if I didn't know about the contents of the flash drive.

I could see the validity of that. But it did make me feel like the hapless, helpless female with bubbles for brains. Though to be fair, I'm not sure I really wanted to know.

"Besides, Ava, there wasn't much. And what was there—was a goddamn fucking riddle. But there's no harm in telling you this, Tomi's husband, Brent, was a total prick!" Sage confessed with an aggrieved tone.

Once Sage started driving towards the Palisades, I realized that Sage had changed his mind and we were going to my father's house. A chill of apprehension settled in my bones and I shivered. Ivan had killed my cousin Natalia there.

Was any place safe?

The mountains had been beautiful and safe. Sage and I had solidified our love there, but it had started to feel like a prison. I was more than happy to escape the restrictions. However, I couldn't fool myself into believing that this wasn't just an exchange of one prison for another—albeit all dressed up and sitting in the Palisades.

Alexei was expecting us and opened the door to welcome me home. I stepped into his arms and hugged him back. Though we didn't know each all that well yet, I already felt a paternal love for the man.

Alexei showed us around the house again. I skipped the ballroom where Natalia died, even though it had been renovated. He showed Sage while I waited in the hallway. I should have gone in too, but I just couldn't do it—too many memories.

Alexei wanted me to be comfortable with the layout of the house and he wanted Sage to see the improvements he made to the security system. We both felt more at ease and comfortable by the time we finished the tour.

He brought us to a beautiful suite of rooms on the second floor where he said I would be staying. They comprised one end of the house and afforded me a one hundred and eighty degree view. As such, they overlooked the front, which faced West and the ocean, the grounds to the North, and the gardens and the pool which were located out the back.

"This is far more than I need, Alexei. A bedroom to sleep in would be more than enough." I tried to protest, but he was insistent.

"You'll have these, Ava. I had them designed specifically for you."

And that was the end of the discussion. Arguing would have done me no good and would have changed nothing—stubborn man. They were elegantly decorated. They had been painted in a dove grey color and accented with white and charcoal. They reminded me of Sage's bedroom. There was comfort in that.

The three of us had dinner together and discussed what to expect over the next few weeks and months.

I wasn't happy about any of it. But I tried to be understanding of their rules and their need to protect me. And Sage's need to go under again to investigate this Dark folder that Tomi had left for him.

He owed it to her memory. I kept telling myself that. Over and over.

Tomi was haunting our present and she would continue to haunt our future, if Sage didn't resolve the mystery of her and the Dark folder. He needed the resolution so that he could put her in the past—where she belonged.

"Ava, I have a few things I wanted to discuss with you and Sage," Alexei told me, then continued on to say, "though Sage knows most of this already."

I looked over to Sage and he nodded—a look of remorse on his face. I knew they had chatted during Sage's recovery and they had kept in contact while we were in the mountains. But I didn't realize they were sharing confidences. I felt a bit betrayed.

"I have to tell you a story first. It's about your mother, Grace. We didn't have the opportunity to talk about this before you had to leave."

"I know that you loved her and me. I don't doubt that at all."

"I did love you both and would have done anything to protect you and Grace," he paused, visibly collecting himself. "But I failed to protect my Grace and because of that—you lost your mother and your grandparents."

"Alexei, you can't blame yourself for their car accident. Not to be flippant, but accidents do happen."

"Well, you see, Ava," he paused, then swallowed, "that's not entirely true."

Looking straight at me, he proceeded to lay bare the classified, yet uncensored truths about his youth and the death of my mother, Grace.

# CHAPTER TWENTY

# Ava

"I met Grace when she was dancing for the New York City Ballet, that much you know. It truly was love at first sight," Alexei stated simply.

"Yes, I remember you telling me that when we first met at The Shrine. You said that I reminded you of a dancer you had once known—my mother. I couldn't believe that someone in LA knew her. Only Chloe had ever talked to me about my mother. Of course, I had no idea just how well you knew her and me."

"And I'm sorry for that. You dance just like her, Ava and with the same exquisite grace."

"I used to dance that way," I said, with a sigh of acceptance, "but I'm different now and so is my dancing."

"You're still exceptional and will continue to be so. Don't lose faith in that, Ava."

I nodded, as I didn't think I could speak at that moment. His and Sage's faith in me were unwavering. Sage grabbed for my hand and held it firmly while Alexei continued his story.

"I loved your mother almost from the moment that I met her, but it was hard to believe that she could love me too. I was just a gutter rat from Russia."

Alexei explained how as a young man fresh from Russia, he had nothing and no one to rely upon. He was recruited by a Russian guy working for an organization Alexei had later dubbed the Brotherhood. They dealt in various black market activities, including human trafficking, he admitted.

"I had my strength and if I were being honest, my very agile mind. The combination had taken me far within the organization. But this was not the kind of life I had wanted when defecting to the US. It wasn't the career I aspired to have."

"How could you be involved in something like that?"

"At first I thought it was just sex clubs—consensual clubs—however, I came to realize it was so much more than that. And I didn't want to be associated with them anymore, especially not after I met your mother."

Grace changed his whole world and he wanted to make a clean break and go legit. He worked quietly towards that goal for years. But when he was finally ready to make a break, he feared the organization wouldn't allow it.

"The head of the organization somehow realized I was going to leave. So I was sent to LA to assess the possibility for expansion of our black market activities to the West coast. And that trip was the beginning of the end," he told us, sadness ripe in his voice.

"Before I left, I remember watching you and your mother sleeping. You were wrapped around each other cuddling and sleeping the sleep of the innocent. I thought how I would never sleep like that. I felt too tainted by all that I had been associated with. If I had only known then that they were going to kill Grace and steal you away from me, I would have walked away from you and your mother—just to keep you safe. I hope you believe that."

"What do you mean Grace was killed and I was stolen? Chole adopted me when my family died in that car accident. What aren't you telling me?" I demanded, as various scenarios ran through my mind. I felt nauseous at his implications.

"I originally thought Grace and her parents had died in a car accident and they did, yet not exactly," he paused for a moment before continuing. "Ivan was the one who told me about the car accident when I returned from LA. But I had no idea where you were, Ava and neither did Ivan. I never found you, despite looking endlessly for years. You were just gone."

The pain in that last statement was palpable. But at the mention of Ivan's name, I had more questions. "How would Ivan know about Grace? I thought you said you kept us a secret, as much as possible."

"I did, but Ivan was my right-hand-man. He knew almost everything. I regret that he did, more than you could possibly know. My association with him and the Brotherhood cost me your mother and you. The two most important things in my life."

Alexei went on to tell me how after identifying my mother at the coroner's office, he had been approached by a man with information about her death...

*When I left the coroner's office, I had left my heart behind with Grace. Stepping outside, I wondered how the sun could possibly be shining, when I was in such a dark place. I was numb, but not so lost in my head that I didn't realize I was being followed. I had thought to just play along—feign stupidity. I wasn't in the mood for a confrontation.*

*I continued walking down the street and my tail kept pace. Up the street and around the corner, I ducked into an alley and waited. Deciding to force an encounter, I wanted to be done with this nonsense. If blood were to be shed, then all the better. I wanted to be with my Grace anyway.*

*I didn't have to wait long, as a man in his early fifties came into the alley with me. I continued to lean against the brick wall, arms crossed at my chest. There would be no stopping whatever was about to go down.*

*"Alexei Vinokourov, we've been watching you for some time now. I'm Bradley, Sean Bradley," he stated while reaching out his empty hand to shake mine.*

*Not what I had been expecting.*

*"I have some information I'd like to share with you—regarding Grace Leclair."*

*Now he had my undivided attention. Straightening from the wall, I shook his hand and I stood directly in front of this Bradley, waiting.*

*"We've been watching you for some time. Following your movements. We know about your recent trip to LA for Maxim. We also know about your disillusionment, your quiet efforts to escape Maxim's yoke. Just as we know about your efforts to rescue some of the young women you've found trapped within the sex trade."*

*My head was reeling, but I didn't let that show. How could this, 'we' know of my efforts? I had been very careful about secreting these women away. I didn't say anything, but rather just waited.*

"We know about Grace and Ava, though you have been very good at keeping them hidden."

Bradley stopped talking and looked around before staring directly into my eyes saying, "What we know is that someone inside Maxim's organization killed Grace and her parents—at Maxim's direction. It was not an accident as you were led to believe."

The numbness in which I'd been immersed was swiftly replaced by a raging inferno of emotions.

I'd heard the term, 'seeing red,' but hadn't understood until just that moment what it felt like. I was lost in a maelstrom until Bradley hit my jaw with a resounding thud, snapping me from the mental chaos.

"Are you with me now? They made it look like an accident, but it wasn't. We had a guy watching Grace. She and her parents were on their way to a girlfriend's house, where Ava had been playing. They were deliberately run off the road. Our man could do nothing to stop what happened, it was so unexpected. He rendered aid at the scene, but to no avail."

I honestly didn't know how to react to that. I wanted to commit murder and I was more than ready to hunt down the fucker that had taken my beloved away from me. I needed to cut the head off of the proverbial snake—Maxim. However, Bradley stopped me in my tracks with one simple question.

"If I could guarantee you Maxim and no jail time, would you consider working for us?" He held up his hand to prevent me from answering, as if I would need think about that question. I would take whatever was offered to see him dead. Hell, I would sell my very soul to avenge my Grace.

*"We have also taken the liberty to hide Ava from those who would seek to do her harm." With that final statement, it didn't matter what I would have done because I would do anything for my Ava.*

"I've been undercover since that day—working for a covert branch of the FBI. We have been quietly trying to put a stop to human trafficking. We've had some great successes but more failures than should have been possible. There is something more going on here—some other organization that is running the show from behind a veil of secrecy. We've been looking for ways to unmask them all these long years."

"You knew about all of this?" I asked Sage.

He nodded. "Only recently, Beauty and not all of it. Alexei confessed some of it before you and I fled LA. He wanted to be sure that I realized how much deeper the investigation went. And he wanted me to know that we were on the same team. For years the LAPD thought Alexei was the mastermind behind the human trafficking ring. Ivan and his cronies did an exceptional job of deflecting."

"Ivan acted subservient, but he wasn't." Alexei said, "It was all an act. I would've never believed that he had the intelligence to pull this off."

"We now realize that Ivan had to be the head guy. He has been setting up Alexei as their fall guy all along. But what he didn't realize was that Alexei had traded sides." Sage added.

"Alexei? This Bradley guy promised you Maxim, which meant what? And you said he stole me away. How could you possibly have trusted anything he told you?" Surely I wasn't the only one who thought this was all suspect.

"First of all, he gave you to Chole and arranged for you guys to move away to Palm Springs. Safe and far away from the danger in New York. It would appear to everyone that I was deeply involved in the organization. That would have made you a target. My new enemies would've stopped at nothing to use you as leverage against me. Just like Bradley did, by stealing you away. He knew I would do anything to keep you safe."

"But what about Maxim? Who was he and what did you do with him?"

"I didn't do anything with him, the FBI did. They put him away for life and I took his place as head of the organization. Or so the underworld thought."

"So for all these years you've had to play at being the leader in charge of this Russian underworld and its black market activity?" I asked, thinking how awful it must have been to do things you didn't agree with or want to do, but did anyways—all for the greater good.

"I wouldn't say that I've *played* at it, but rather, I've owned that role. I'm not proud of some of the things I've had to do and believe me, I've done more than my fair share of bad things. I'm no Boy Scout, Ava."

I knew what he was doing and I wasn't buying it. He thought to paint himself as less than what he was—a hero—like Sage. Both of my men had been forced to do things they didn't want to—all in the hopes that they would eventually stop the madness and save a life or two. Sacrificing themselves and their happiness was an acceptable payment for their imagined sins.

I would show them both that I understood and loved them regardless. "Okay, thank you for telling me all of this. But why did Maxim have my mother killed? What was the purpose?"

"There was no purpose to it that I could see and have come to believe that he wasn't responsible."

"Who then? And why?"

"Ivan. I truly believe it was Ivan."

# CHAPTER TWENTY-ONE

# Ava

After dinner, Sage and I went for a walk through the gardens.

I was still off balance from the conversation with my father and his revelations. Ivan, always Ivan destroying my life and that of my loved ones. I couldn't fathom why he would kill my mother. It made no sense.

Could there ever be a reason that was good enough to kill an innocent woman and her parents—leaving an orphaned daughter? Should I have died in that car too? Had that actually been his plan? Would he have killed me in that warehouse if given the chance?

I think he would have raped and then killed me without a doubt. Sage and Alexei had saved me from that eventuality.

Now Sage had to leave me to go undercover again. He felt duty bound to investigate the death of Tomi's daughter and that of her husband. He seemed to think that Ivan was involved, which made sense considering he had set up Alexei as the perpetrator. And we knew that he wasn't the one responsible.

So now we had to say goodbye so that Sage could leave me and go face unknown dangers.

How do we do that? How do we say goodbye, when it could be for the last time?

"I can't do it, Sage. I can't say goodbye," I said, my voice raw with emotion and unshed tears.

"Then don't. Let's just say, I love you and I'll see you again."

"I do love you," I told him simply.

But it felt as if I wouldn't be able to breathe without him standing next to me. We had become so close over the past three months that I couldn't even fathom going days without seeing him.

Not again.

"How will I breathe?" Slipped out before I could stop it. I didn't want to appear weak or clinging.

"Come here, Beauty," he said and pulled me into his arms.

I rested my head on his chest and listened as his heart spoke to me. It was soothing and steady, just like Sage. But I was feeling decidedly unsteady and lost.

"Do you remember when we were on the beach and I asked you to step into the darkness with me?"

"Yes, I do."

"Let me remind you of what I said...

*Ava, I know your emotions are chaotic and everything seems out of control, but you'll get back to the life you had, to the dreams you made. I promise this is only temporary. I want more than anything for you to have your heart's desires; your happiness is what matters to me. Before I met you, Beauty, I had no idea I could love this way, this desperately, this completely—this hard. You broke through my defenses to invade my darkness, Ava, you've nestled in so deep, I don't think my soul could breathe without you.*

"So you see, I need you to breathe as well. We'll make it through this, Beauty, just have faith."

God, I loved him so much. How will I live without him?

"Can we see each other while you're undercover?"

I couldn't look at him when he answered. I didn't want to see the answer in his eyes. And I didn't want him to see the pain in mine.

But he gave me no choice. He cradled my face and lifted my gaze to his, so that we were looking at each other.

"No. Because I don't want to lead Ivan and his goons here. To you."

I could see the regret in his eyes, but the determination as well. He needed to do right by Tomi and her daughter Emma. I wouldn't stand in his way. Even though I was so scared for his safety.

Ivan had shot and nearly killed him once before. He could do it again. What if next time Sage didn't make it? My heart skipped a beat at the thought.

"I don't want to leave you here, Ava, believe me. I would rather be the one protecting you. I wish we could have stayed in the mountains or gone somewhere else."

"I know. But you have to solve this mystery and finally lay Tomi's ghost to rest."

I'll be strong for Sage, I told myself. I will give him my love and support, not my fears and doubts. I will leave him with the image of my strength and my undying love. A warrior Princess to my tarnished, but steadfast knight.

I would channel her strength and own that persona. Even when on the inside I felt so small and so alone. I wouldn't let him see how I was hurting.

"You will come back to me, Sage. Do you hear me?" I said desperately. "I will accept nothing less than you here and in my arms again."

"That's a promise. I'll come back to you."

He pulled me into his arms and kissed me deeply, fusing our mouths and imprinting my body with his. I didn't want to let go and clung to him—gripping his arms hard enough to bruise.

My heart was breaking, but I refused to show it.

"I want you, Sage. Now!"

I pulled him around to the back of the pool house and out of view of the main house. It felt like we were sneaking around like naughty children. Once there, I slipped off my undies and lifted my skirt. Sage was on board and had unzipped his jeans.

"Now. I need you right now!"

"Let me kiss you again."

Thinking he meant to claim my mouth, my breath caught when he dropped his knees before me and kissed my clitoris.

"Fuck!" I cried out. He gave me no quarter and within minutes I was coming against his talented tongue.

"Please," I begged.

"Come here, you," Sage said, as he pulled his cock out of his jeans and turned me to face the wall.

"Fast and furious. Here you go," he said before he slowly slid into me from behind.

I was bent at the waist with my hands against the wall for support. Sage was sliding in and out at an excruciatingly slow pace. His hands were gripping my hips. Sage grunted in pleasure as I rose up onto the balls of my feet for added leverage and increased depth.

Every slow thrust was calculated and measured to give us the most pleasure. I lifted my right leg up and wrapped it around Sage's hip. He held my thigh in his right hand and my hip in the other. The added depth just about sent us over the edge, but we held off—not wanting this to end.

I bit my lip hard enough to taste blood. I was trying to be quiet and fight my impending orgasm. But I couldn't hold it off, Sage wouldn't let me.

"You will come for me, Ava. Now!"

As always, I did as he commanded my body and happily so.

"I want to feel you, Sage. I mean it. Hard and fast. Right now!"

He gave me what I wanted and we gloriously orgasmed in synchronicity. Afterwards, I stood up and Sage turned me around to devour my mouth again. I could feel him everywhere—in me, on me, and surrounding me—I didn't want to lose those feelings.

"I have to go, Ava," He told me as I slipped my undies back on.

"I know."

We walked towards the house and in through the french doors. He hugged me again.

"Will you walk me out to the front?"

"Let's say, *I will see you later* from here. I can't watch you leave."

Strong! I was strong. I wouldn't cry. Warrior Princess! I kept telling myself, while my nails dug crescents into my palms.

"Okay, Beauty. I love you. And I *will* see you later," he said and kissed me one last time before turning to go.

I ran up the stairs to my new room. I could watch Sage leave from there. But I wouldn't, I told myself. But then changed course and ran to the window. The lights were out in my room. I would be hidden, and Sage wouldn't be able to see that I watched him go.

I pressed my palm against the window when I saw him open the car door and get inside. He sat there for a few minutes before he finally left.

Did he see me watching him? Was he contemplating a life without me, like I was imagining one without him?

I stayed strong for Sage. I was proud of myself because he would carry a vision of me with my head held high and poised.

A warrior Princess.

I crawled into my lonely bed with its cold sheets and laid onto my side. Grabbing the spare pillow, I hugged it tight. Biting into the pillow helped to muffle the sobs that shook my body, while the pillowcase under my cheek helped to soak up my tears.

Please, I prayed, keep Sage safe and bring him home to me.

# CHAPTER TWENTY-TWO

# Ava

So here I was ghosting about my father's house trying to be comfortable in a space that was not my own. I should be used to this unsettled feeling of displacement by now, but I wasn't.

Alexei was in his office, and I was standing before his black-and-white photos that lined the hallway. I had first seen them at the party he had thrown for me after my solo debut. Before all hell broke loose; before my cousin was shot and killed; before Sage and I had fled LA.

As I studied each photo I tried to understand the many facets of this man who was my father. Most children had a lifetime to learn and to know these things about their parents. Their vision of them changing through the years as they grew from childhood wonder to the acceptance and understanding that comes with age, wisdom, and adulthood. I was on the crash-course version to understanding and without the rose-colored lenses of youth.

Those lenses had been ripped off last night during our dinner conversation. But in the light of day, I still found him to be a hero. Though it was clear to me that he wouldn't classify himself as such.

According to Sage and my father, I wasn't supposed to go anywhere, talk to anyone, or see any of my friends. However, now that I was back home in LA, I knew with a certainty that I wouldn't be able to comply with their wishes.

I needed to dance. I needed to see my friends. I needed to have a life, because living like this was no life at all. It meant that the bad guys were winning. That they were controlling my every move, my every breath, just as they consumed my every thought.

Enough was enough.

I walked to the bedroom that I was occupying on the second floor and decided to call Willow.

To hell with it!

"Hello." Willow said or asked, depending on how you viewed it.

"Willow?" I whispered despite the fact that nobody was in the room with me. Who did I think was going to hear me? "Hi honey, it's me, Ava."

"Oh my God, oh my God, oh my God! Hold on, okay?"

I held my phone away from my ear and turned my head to look at it. Did she seriously just ask me to hold on? We hadn't spoken in over three months and she tells me to hold on.

Good Lord.

I put the phone back up to my ear. I could hear her fumbling around. Whatever she was doing was extremely loud. Then I heard her yelling for Daniel at a decibel high enough to break my eardrum. But I smiled to myself. I could hear the excited emotion lacing her voice as she called out to Daniel. She really was the best girlfriend ever.

"Ava? Are you there? Are you really there?" she asked with obvious emotion.

"I'm really here. I came back to LA yesterday. I'm so glad that Daniel is with you. It's like a twofer," I said with a huge smile.

"We have so much to talk about. I want to hear all about what has been going on for the past three months that Sage and I have been away. But I don't want to talk over the phone, just in case," I said with warning.

"What's going on? Are you still in danger? I thought you weren't coming back to LA until all of that crazy business had been resolved. Should you be calling me? What if someone's listening? Ava..." Willow asked in one run on question.

"Honey, take a breath. I'm okay. I'm safe. Everything is going to be all right," I said trying to convince myself as well as Willow.

"Why don't you and Daniel meet me at my favorite eatery tomorrow. You know the one I'm talking about and where. How about at noon? Will that work for the two of you?"

"I asked Daniel. It works just fine for us. Mason is busy with football in San Diego so he won't be able to come tomorrow. Will Sage be there?"

I didn't want to answer her as to what Sage would be doing, so I simply said, "No, not tomorrow."

"Okay. We'll see you tomorrow at noon. At you know where. We want to hear all about what has been going on with you and Sage. Plus, we have lots tell you too."

"Perfect. I'll see you tomorrow."

I wasn't sure if I should congratulate myself for embracing my inner rebel. It seemed wrong to do so, but I just couldn't continue to live this life of oppression—no matter how well-meaning it was. And so, I wouldn't throw a party, but I would celebrate taking this first step towards regaining control over my life.

I had this clawing need within my soul to dance again, but I needed more than just dancing by myself within the confines of a beautiful cabin in the mountains. I was determined to restart my ballet career and move forward with that aspect of my life.

Sage wanted me to stay here with the same type of restrictions as I had in the mountains, but I couldn't do that. To continue on in that way, would mean that Ivan and his goons were winning. It would mean that they had complete control and I was nothing more than their puppet. I wouldn't dance to their tune any longer.

I doubted I would have a chance to dance with the LA Ballet again. I had only been with them for a short time when I left unexpectedly. I'm sure my dependability would be a factor in their decision to allow me to come back or not. I would search for alternatives so that I could continue to pursue my dream of being a professional dancer.

I wouldn't let them win. I wouldn't let Ivan destroy the dreams that I had worked my entire life to achieve. Dreams that would honor my mother Grace and my mother Chloe. It was in their memory that I would continue to pursue my passion—no matter what.

I just hoped that Sage would understand.

# CHAPTER TWENTY-THREE

# Sage

"What do you mean she's not there?" I yelled into the phone. "You had one job, Alexei. Just one. To watch your daughter. To keep her there. To keep her safe. How fucking hard is it?"

What was I thinking? I should have never brought Ava to her father's house. I wanted to be the one protecting her, but I couldn't be undercover and watch her at the same time. So I trusted Alexei to keep her safe for me. He had failed in his one task.

"She was here this morning when I left for a meeting. Not once over breakfast did she indicate she was going out or going anywhere. With all that has been going on, I wouldn't have expected her to leave the house. I'm just as surprised as you are."

"How long do you think she's been gone?"

"My best guess? No more than a couple of hours."

I turned my wrist so I that could see the time—half past two in the afternoon. It felt much later. The smoke-filled dive where I was holed-up didn't have proper windows to allow for light to filter in. Which was probably a good thing—that way no one could examine the environment too closely.

Brent had mentioned a guy in the Dark folder—saying that he occasionally came to this hole-in-the-wall dive to get his drink on. But that was over five years ago. I doubted that this stake out would lead to anything, but I had to try.

He was one of the few cryptic bits of information that Brent had provided. Or misinformation that he had planted—depending on how it played out.

Brent had alleged that this guy was up to his ass in human trafficking. That he was known for his connections with hardcore kink and sex slavery. I wondered why Brent would give up this information. The only answers I had so far, were written in that file.

*I may have fallen into the Dark by happenstance, or by greed—what I like to call opportunistic blackmail—but I hate the abuse of power. I hate cops and you in particular. But I especially hate dirty cops who hide behind their badges abusing their power.*

Fuck!

"Give me ten minutes. In the meantime, don't you have video surveillance? Check that. See how she left and with whom."

"Seriously? I checked that before I called you."

"And?" I said with obvious impatience.

"Uber for God's sake?"

"What?"

"That crazy girl left with an Uber driver. Willingly. What the hell was she thinking?"

"Five minutes and I'm on my way," I said, as I hung up on Alexei and stood to leave.

I had just pulled my wallet out to pay, when the front door opened and afternoon sun filtered into the darkness—illuminating all that should have remained hidden.

I couldn't see who it was and didn't really care because I was leaving. But as my twenty landed on the sticky bar, my wrist vibrated, as did my phone that was in my pocket. I thought about ignoring it, but with Ava missing, I knew I couldn't.

"What now?" I said to Alexei, who was on the other end.

"Ava just walked in. Stay where you are. She's safe and said that she had lunch with Willow and Daniel. Don't worry, I'll ring her neck for you."

"Tell Ava that I'll be there later, if I can make it."

This day was turning out to be a huge waste of time. And I had a feeling that this would be the norm throughout this case. The *cryptic leads* to *dead-ends* ratio would not be in my favor.

Several hours and many drinks later, I was ready to go. This had been one of those dead-ends and a colossal waste of time. Frustrated, I pivoted to leave and stepped into a puddle of alcohol.

Fuck me running!

Over the hours I had created that puddle with the crappy, bottom-shelf liquor I had been served and had in turn poured it onto the floor.

I spotted who I thought could be my guy based on the description Brent had given me in the file, but people can change a lot in five years. Thinking quick, I made a huge show out of adjusting the boys in my pants and then turned around to sit back down on my bar stool.

I felt like Ivan just then and that was just so wrong. I was convinced that Ivan had some kind of pathologic issue with his constant need to adjust himself. All guys did it, at one time or another, but damn if Ivan didn't adjust himself incessantly.

The guy sat down a few stools away from me, ordered a drink, and lit up a cigarette. California law prohibits smoking inside, but no one would be enforcing that law here. I raised my finger up and nodded towards the barkeep, indicating that I wanted another drink. I might have to actually drink this one in truth.

When another thirty minutes had passed and my guy didn't seem in a hurry to go anywhere or do anything, I decided to hit the restroom. I couldn't have been gone for more than five minutes, if even that; but the landscape within the bar had definitely changed.

I grabbed a table next to the front door instead of going back to the bar. I wanted to keep my back against the wall and my eyes on the two sitting in front of me.

An officer from LAPD had joined my guy at the bar and I couldn't believe who it was, Officer Todd. Or Officer Peacock as Ava liked to call him. He was the detective who had come to Cedars-Sinai to interview her after the rape.

It had felt so good to punch him in the face for how he had treated my Ava. Captain Starnes, my commanding officer, had reached out to the commanding officer of his division, and Officer Peacock had been reprimanded.

Knowing how these things worked, his only reprimand had probably been an online sensitivity training module. But as the saying goes; you can't fix stupid—well, you can't change an asshole either.

I took out a special listening device from my pocket and slipped it into my ear. It would cut down on the ambient noise and allow me to focus on the conversation at the bar. A recording program was connected to my phone and would capture the conversation just in case I couldn't hear it...

"There's a shipment that needs to be picked up two days from now on Friday," Peacock said.

"That's earlier than expected. I have a truck scheduled and ready to go for next week. I'll have to change the date."

"There's also been a change in the destination."

"Oh? And you're just now telling me all of this?"

*My guy didn't sound too happy about the changes.*

"We had a buyer come in at the last minute. He wants everything—site unseen. He said he didn't need to inspect the stock. So this shipment will be headed east to Kansas City, where additional stock is waiting. Then it will head south, down the 35 corridor through Texas and into Mexico. We're cleaning house with this one. That means you'll have to up your game and your acquisitions to restock."

"I've recruited more coeds and some gang members to help with that."

"Perfect."

"But I'm running low on Rohyp and Jet."

*Fuckers! They were talking about trafficking. They had to be.*

"How could you be low on Rohypnol and Ketamine already? I just gave you that large supply I acquired."

*Stole from a drug bust was more like it.*

"I've started collecting more stock in anticipation. That takes more, as does maintaining things at Hotel Dark. Just get me more. I'm not skimming, if that's what you're worried about."

"I'll see what I can do. In the meantime, make sure that this shipment is delivered promptly and without issue. You'll get a bonus if our customer is satisfied."

"Where's this shipment ultimately going? Who's the buyer?"

"That's not information that you need to know to perform your job. Just do what you're told. If you perform it well, you'll get your bonus."

And now I'm thinking—you can't fix stupid, you can't change an asshole, and you can't clean dirty. Once a dirty cop, always a dirty cop. Peacock had to be one of the important ones that Brent had been referring to. The one I needed to follow for now, though maybe not the ultimate secret he alluded to. He couldn't be, though I thought he might be evil. Sadistic and cruel for sure.

Their conversation seemed to be winding down, so I threw some money onto the table and quietly left out the front door.

I slipped my Ray-Bans on—the bright LA sunshine hurt my eyes after having spent hours in that dark hole. I was taking a chance that I could miss some information passed between them, but I wanted to be in my car and waiting for them to leave.

I really needed to follow both guys. I grabbed my phone.

"Carter, I need you at this address in ten minutes." I gave him the address. "Can you manage it?"

"On my way. At the studio now, so that's close by."

"Follow the car I tell you to and report back to me where he goes."

"On it. I'm bringing Lilly with me."

"I'm not sure that's a great idea. I shouldn't even be asking your help."

"I've helped you before. I'll help you again. Don't worry about it."

"Thanks."

"No thanks are needed. We wanted to go for a drive anyway," Carter said with obvious humor.

I was breaking rules and going against what I knew to be right by having Carter help me. But I didn't know what else to do. I couldn't very well follow both of them.

I didn't have much to go on, but if I were to gather some relevant evidence I would reach out to Lieut. Clark and update him as to what I was doing and why. I had a feeling I would be needing his assistance at some point.

I texted Ava next, "I love you."

Ava replied, "I'm sorry, I love you too.

"Glad you're safe," I told her.

"I didn't mean to worry you," she said.

"I can't come over. I don't want to put you at risk," I texted.

"I know," she told me.

"Please be careful, Beauty and stay at Alexei's," I instructed.

"I'll try," Ava texted.

"I have to go, please be safe," I begged her.

"You too," was her final reply.

I couldn't really blame Ava for wanting to see her friends. Daniel was like a brother to her and Willow was the sister she'd always wanted. But the fact that Ivan was running around loose worried me constantly. Thankfully, he didn't know that we were in town—or I hoped he didn't.

I was keeping an eye on the front door and the surrounding area for Carter. My phone buzzed with an incoming text from Carter. They were down the street. He said he could see my rental car and the front door to the bar.

A short time later, Peacock strutted his way out. I really wanted to knock the smugness right off his face and told myself I'd find a way to do just that.

The sun would be setting soon and darkness would fall over LA—which could make following these guys simultaneously easier and more difficult. Easier to shield our identities, but perhaps more difficult to hide the fact that we were following them.

I felt compelled to text a few instructions to Carter about the best way to keep a tail on this guy without being caught. I chuckled to myself when he responded with the word "No," sitting right next to the poop emoji. I could always count on Carter to find a way to make me laugh when things got overly crazy.

Peacock lit up a cigarette, took a deep drag, then appeared to be staring at the glowing tip as he exhaled.

I'll never forget how he had come to the hospital to interview Ava. He had been a complete condescending asshole—but she had used her height to tower over him. She had told Peacock what she thought about his questions and their implications.

He wasn't a very tall guy, perhaps five-foot-five or six, barrel chested, and sporting a spare tire around the middle. He clearly suffered from short man syndrome and ticked off every box related to it—and he was a dirty cop to boot. He abused the badge and the power that came with it.

He took another drag of his cigarette, threw the butt onto the ground, and stepped on it as he walked towards his car.

I grabbed my cell phone.

"I'm out. Keep me posted on things. Your dude just walked out the door."

"We're on it."

I would have to trust Carter to be smart and to keep safe. So I put Carter and Lilly out of my mind and focused on Peacock as he drove through the streets of LA.

# CHAPTER TWENTY-FOUR

# Sage

Following that douche-bag Peacock around LA sucked, but it had to be done. I didn't know his personal information and couldn't access it through police channels without alerting someone.

He was all over LA, with no real destination that I could determine. He stopped at the roach-coach along Pico, close to Fairfax, and grabbed some dinner. The aroma of carne asada and fresh lime made my mouth water. I could kill the fat-fuck for taunting me with his street tacos—I was starving.

If I didn't know better, I would think that he had figured out that I was following him and stopped at random places just to be a prick. But I did know better. He was just that oblivious and too self-absorbed to recognize that he had a tail. How he had remained undetected as a dirty cop was hard to believe, but I'd seen stranger things.

"Please tell me that you guys are having better luck than I am," I said without preamble after dialing Carter.

"That bad, eh?"

"So far he's stopped for dinner, picked up some dry cleaning, and now he's at a pastry shop. I swear if he walks out with a box of donuts I will not be responsible for the kill shot placed between his eyes."

Carter's laughter echoed through the phone and I heard Lilly laughing after his verbatim recitation of what I had just said.

"If you're done laughing at that stereotypical asshat, tell what you've got," I said with a chuckle.

"Not much. Though our guy visited a shipping yard —a rental-type place offering both aquatic and land transportation. It looks like you can rent just transportation from them, or hire out the whole enchilada, which includes a driver and transpo. Or that's what their website said."

"Text the address. Are you still on him?"

"We are."

"Okay. I'll check back in later. But if something comes up before then, reach out."

"Will do."

Since Peacock was still in the pastry shop chatting, I googled the shipping yard that Carter mentioned. Was he arranging for the transportation of drugs or humans? Whichever the case, they needed to be stopped—and by Friday. Deep in my gut, I knew that time was of the essence and I needed backup. I sent off a quick text to the Lieut.

*Back in LA.*

*Something big is about to go down.*

*It involves the mystery surrounding Tomi.*

*I'll send more details later.*

*Look into Officer Todd, on the down-low.*

Peacock had finally shut his yapping pie hole and walked out of the bakery carrying a box that looked suspiciously like donuts. You have got to be kidding me. Could he be any more of a walking cliché?

I followed him for a few more hours. He dropped the donuts off downtown where his unit was located—which made me suspicious. What was he picking up—more drugs? He drove home after that, so all-in-all it had been extremely boring and nothing more had been gained.

I sent a follow up text to the Lieut. telling him that I needed someone to tail Peacock because I had some-where else to go tonight.

*On it.*

*I expect answers, Detective.*

*Relief will be there in twenty.*

I read between the lines of that text. The Lieut. was not happy for being late to the party. I would have to smooth things over later. He'd understand once I ex-plained the events of the past two days. Or had it been three now? I shook my head, just two.

Exactly twenty minutes later my relief showed up. I filled James in on the details and what I needed. I trust-ed him and knew he'd keep me informed. The Lieut. had sent another man to spell Carter and Lilly. I'd defi-nitely catch hell over having civilians involved.

I'd worry about the repercussions of that later, for now I had another lead from the Dark folder to follow.

# CHAPTER TWENTY-FIVE

# Ava

It was Friday night and I was sneaking out of my father's house—again, though I didn't exactly sneak out the last time. I had just left without telling anyone where I was going. Not really the same thing, or so I kept telling myself. But this time, I really was sneaking out.

I felt more like a rebellious teen than the adult I was. But I wanted to see Willow and Daniel play at Club Nitro downtown—so I was going, even though I promised Alexei that I wouldn't sneak out again.

I was determined to take my life back.

The last time, on Wednesday, I had left the house to meet Willow and Daniel for lunch. Alexei just happened to be away at a meeting, which wasn't my fault, but I should have texted or called him. But I knew how that conversation would have played out—so I'd skipped the inevitable argument.

As I left my father's house, I wondered whether Alexei and Sage would forgive me this time. Would they understand my need to be strong, even though I was still scared?

I would be with friends. I wouldn't be drinking anything. What could go wrong?

I should have known better than to even think that
question, now it was out there in the universe—waiting.

***

At lunch on Wednesday, the three of us took turns
detailing all that had happened over the past three
months. There were times that Willow and Daniel
stumbled over each other. They tried to tell me everything all at once and in one breath.

"Willow and I started playing the club scene."

"When Daniel withdrew from law school."

"The sudden lack of funds made continuing at
UCLA impossible. That had been an unexpected blow.
Yet it wasn't at all surprising, just disappointing. Re-
gardless, I was scrambling to adjust," Daniel explained.

"We met here a few months ago," Willow smiled
happily, "to make plans for our club gigs."

"My sudden lack of tuition money was a minor thing
in the grand scheme of life. I mean, how many kids
could say their parents paid for their entire college edu-
cation? I just needed to regroup, refocus, and look for a
plan B or possibly C," he told us with honest humility.

"However, I wouldn't change the fact that I told
them about Mason and I-- there was freedom and peace
in that." Daniel said, before he laid it all out there—raw
and bare.

I listened intently to what Daniel told me, but I kept
looking around. I tried not to be obvious about it. But it
felt like someone was watching me. I knew I must be

imagining things, because no one knew we were in LA. I hated this, as I refocused on what Daniel was telling me.

"It all started with my decision to drive out to the desert to see my parents..."

*I drove out to Palm Springs alone. I didn't want to tell Mason I was going to see my parents. I knew he would want to be with me when I had this conversation with my parents. But I needed to address them alone and in person.*

*Besides, he was in San Diego, where he'd been drafted to play for the Chargers. I didn't want to disrupt his training or game mindset.*

*It had been a wasted trip in any regard. Halfway through my impassioned talk, my father stood up and left the room.*

*I watched him leave.*

*Turning back to my mother, I finished telling her about Mason and I. And while she did listen intently, she hadn't said a word.*

*I left disheartened, yet not surprised.*

*Mason and I had been best friends since we were kids. And we still were.*

*Though now—now we were exploring the potential for more.*

*But the final blow had come a day later—by phone. My father didn't even have the balls to address me in person.*

*The conversation played out exactly as I expected. But it was still painful regardless of my prediction. No yelling or recriminations were offered. Just cold precision with the final verdict delivered.*

*Yelling would have taken emotional investment. And my father could claim neither emotion, nor investment in his eldest son.*

*He informed me, quite clinically, that he spoke for both my mother and himself. That the final decision had been made together. I was disappointed that my mother was in agreement, yet I wasn't surprised.*

*His personality had always dominated hers. He reveled in providing her with the opinions she was allowed.*

*In his narrow, rigid mind, I was beneath his notice and not worth his time.*

*My parents would no longer consider me to be a part of the Creighton family. My own flesh and blood regarded me as less than nothing. Luckily, my younger brother was up north attending Stanford. Away from the family drama, as it were.*

*And it wasn't as if Mason and I didn't have enough battles to overcome on our own. Gay people were hated and reviled in virtually every nation across the world. But now I could add being disowned by my own parents.*

*Thankfully, I favored my mother in looks and not my father. It would have sucked to look at my reflection every day and see my father's bigoted face etched upon mine and staring back at me.*

"Given that my parents had cut me off, I had no choice but to withdraw from UCLA. Federal student aid would be difficult, if not impossible to obtain. Especially given that my parents claimed me on their tax return. Applying for aid for this semester was out of the question."

When I started to speak, Daniel held up his hand—interrupting me. He knew exactly what I was going to say.

"Yes, to answer the question in your eyes. If I had told Mason, he would have given me the money to continue school. And to pay my half of the bills. But that wasn't going to happen. Call it pride, call it stubborn—I don't care what you called it. But I won't tell him. I won't ask for money. Hell to the no!" He finished with a narrowing of his hazel eyes, then quietly said, "sorry," and looked away.

"I understand, Daniel, but what does Mason have to say about all this now?"

Daniel's tortured gaze returned to mine and he shook his head, "I haven't told him."

"When Daniel called me, it couldn't have been more perfect in timing. I was miserable," Willow said as she continued the story.

"After I worked through the emotional fallout, I called Willow. There was no sense in dragging her down into my emotional darkness," Daniel explained somberly.

He reached out and lightly punched her arm before continuing, "Besides, I had hatched a plan while working through my shit and Willow and her mad violin skills were an integral part of my plan's success. I prayed she would embrace my crazy."

"Daniel saved me from a life of monochromatic monotony and well he knows it."

"When I was moping around the house, floundering as to what to do with my life, I began thinking about what Sage had said to Willow and I that day at the beach in Santa Monica."

Willow went on to explain, "like Daniel, I had obsessed over that one little statement offered so casually by Sage. In my mind, the key to being a successful violinist meant I had to play in an orchestra. That was my benchmark."

"But what if we could do something with our music? I kept thinking. What if I could find a way to pay for my half of the bills?" Daniel interjected.

"As you know, Ava, Daniel and I played a lot of club and fraternity gigs during our years at USC. We built a nice fan base and made some good cash. I could see the potential of his plan when it was all laid out. This was the motivation and the excuse I needed to leave the orchestra."

"We don't know whether to thank Sage or to curse him for planting those musical seeds."

"You see, I was stifled riding that orchestral first chair. I was suffocating under all those rules and traditions. I'm not a conformist kind of a girl. I mean look at me," Willow said with a tilt of her chin.

"I have a pierced nose and multiple tattoos. Not really your typical first chair squatter. But in all honesty, I loved the music that Daniel and I made together when we were playing the club scene," Willow finished with an endearing, beatific smile.

"So Willow and I met up a week later to hash out all the details."

"You can't imagine how we talked over one another..."

"And bounced ideas off each other," Daniel finished.

"Oh, I can imagine," I said deadpan, then laughed at the look on their faces.

Willow and Daniel had uploaded some of their music onto Soundcloud for their fans to download. A way to spread the word and gain support.

They were hitting lots of clubs, but some catered to a select type of clientele. Those paid well, Daniel told me, but he worried about Willow's safety. She wasn't worried at all, but then she was carefree and just a bit wild.

None of them are like that Club M, Daniel assured me. Though he did admit that there were some less than legal back room activities going on. They tended to stay in the main gathering areas though, where the dancing and drinks were located.

I had loved seeing them again and missed them so much while I was away. I hoped to see Mason and Riley soon too.

I hadn't planned to talk about the engagement, but Willow was all over my ring.

"Um, Ava?" She questioned while twirling her finger and pointing at my engagement ring. "Do you have something to share, now that we aren't hogging up the conversation?" Willow ended with her eyes all but bugging out of her head and her eyebrows disappearing into her hairline.

I laughed so loud at her antics. I loved that girl.

"We want to hear about it. As your brother, I demand to know the details. Or most of them, that is," Daniel chimed in.

I told them how we had stopped at the beach on our way to the mountains. I needed walk along the sand. I

needed the breeze to wash away the grief and fear clinging to me.

"We had stopped to look out over the water," I told
them, "when Sage pulled me into his arms and held me.
It was so peaceful with the moon shimmering across the
surface, like liquefied moonbeams. We stood there
bathed in moonlight and the gentle breeze. A sense of
tranquility washed over me—whisking away my grief."

"That sounds beautiful," Willow said.

"But then Sage shocked the hell out of me. He
dropped to his knees before me in the sand and asked
me to be his wife."

I smiled at their twin expressions. "Yes, there was
more to his proposal than that, but I'm not sharing
those details."

They understood and didn't press me for more. I
looked off to my left, scanning the people, but nothing
seemed off or out of the ordinary. I decided it was time
to leave. I wanted the safety of Alexei's home. Or better
yet, Sage's arms.

I hugged them both goodbye and told them I would
see them on Friday.

"I can't wait to hear you guys play!"

"We'll come pick you up," Daniel offered.

"No, I'll just meet you guys there," I told them and
went out to grab my Uber home.

My cheeks hurt from our laughter and I was still
smiling when I arrived home. My mood quickly sobered
at the disappointment on my father's face when I
opened the front door and saw him standing there.

"Where have you been?" He asked with a curtness I
had yet to hear directed at me.

I tried to explain. But he cut me off, like an errant teenager and dialed Sage.

"He'll try to come by later tonight," he said, after he told Sage to stay wherever he was and ended the call.

Apparently, he and Sage had taken sides against me.

"You must think I am acting childish for leaving the house. But I'm not. I can't live this half-life anymore. If I do, Ivan wins. He's stolen so much already. I won't allow him to steal my future too."

"He's an evil man, Ava. I worked with him for years and thought I knew him. I didn't. He hid behind a mask of subservience—an affectation of stupidity."

Revulsion for his brand of evil caused a cold sweat to coat my palms. "I know exactly what he is—first hand." My throat tight with remembered fear and pain and the unsettling feeling I'd had all day took shape.

"I won't let him control me anymore. Or my life. I want to live. To love. To dance. Why is that too much to ask?"

"Come here," he said, opening his arms.

I walked forward and into my father's embrace. I wouldn't admit it, but I'd been uneasy today.

"I'm sorry I yelled at you."

"I'm sorry I worried you and Sage. That wasn't my intention. I just wanted to visit with my best friends for a few stolen moments."

"I know, honey. We love you. We are just being protective. In the future, if you want to go somewhere, please let me know and I will arrange for a driver. At least that way, Sage and I will know where you are and how you got there. Uber? Really, Ava?"

I looked up at him and into to eyes that mirrored my own, "Hey, there is nothing wrong with their services."

"I agree. The problem is that we have no way of knowing if the driver is legitimate. What if they driver had been sent by Ivan?"

"How would he even know that I'm here? Or in LA?"

"There are hundreds of ways he could know. That's why we were so worried."

"Sage took precautions to get me here. I just didn't think he would know. Naive on my part. I trust in Sage's abilities."

"And you should. But, we shouldn't take anything for granted. You can't be too safe. Too cautious."

"Okay, I won't do that again and I will let you know if I want to go somewhere."

"Thank you."

# CHAPTER TWENTY-SIX

# Ivan

"Boss. We followed her to a place called The Pie Hole. She had lunch with some friends."

"And?"

"She's meeting her friends at Club Nitro on Friday night."

"Perfect."

"She got engaged to that Sage guy."

"Keep me informed," I told them before hanging up.

Well, Friday would be a reckoning day on multiple fronts. I was cleaning house at Hotel Dark and trucking that stock off to my buyer. And Ava would finally be in my hands where she belonged.

She would not escape me this time. I had important plans for her.

It was time for another offering to the Supremacy and the Elders. And I was choosing Ava to be the sacrifice to The Dark.

I'd have to tell her what an honor she was being granted, just before I killed her. Her sacrifice would do a great deal for me and my position within The Dark.

I would finally be given the European status I had aspired to and had secretly coveted for years. Passed over one too many times, in my opinion. But they would take notice of me now and bring me home and into the fold.

We had a room similar to Club M's Luxe room here at Club Nitro, but the Pantheon had a more sinister reputation. I loved that about this room. I would enjoy killing Ava there.

If I could just find Lilly Blue and kill her and Ava together. Now *that* would be the ultimate sacrifice and would net me a profound reward. My elevation in the Dark would be a given.

"Yosef," I yelled out, knowing he would hear me.

"Yes, Sir?"

"I want you to try to find Lilly again. Try looking at that tattoo studio where Ava and Sage stopped when they arrived in LA. The one where she was originally found. See if that Carter James character knows anything."

"Yes, Sir," he told me, before turning to leave. He was ever the dutiful servant.

"Yosef?" I called out again.

"Yes?"

"Bring me that new acquisition. The one with the brunette hair and the pale skin, Hannah I think. I need her," I told him, as I rubbed my hardening cock.

"Yes, Sir. I shall return."

Anticipation was truly the best aphrodisiac a person could have. Fucking this new girl would be a poor substitute for Ava, but they did look similar.

I knew I should allow the anticipation to mount over the next couple of days. But I also knew I wouldn't. I wanted relief and I wanted it now.

I would have to make a concerted effort not to kill this one. A useless waste if I did—especially when I could be paid a bit of money for her. Maybe I would though. It would appease the beast, at least until I got my hands on Ava. Perhaps I would after all.

Yosef knocked and entered. He had the girl by the wrist and was dragging her in behind him. She was wide-eyed, frightened, and completely aware.

Perfect.

# CHAPTER TWENTY-SEVEN

# Ava

When my Uber pulled up to the old, run down building where I was meeting Willow and Daniel, I almost told the driver to turn around and go home. But I wanted to see them play.

Taking a deep breath, I paid and walked with determined strides through the entrance. Once inside, every step felt like I was heading in the wrong direction and the twentieth floor would be a long way from the exit.

Once at the club's entrance, I paid my twenty bucks to enter. The jacked-up meathead at the club door gave me the creeps with his leering stare. Walking straight over to the stage where Willow and Daniel were set up, I waved and smiled up at my besties. I had made it just in time.

"Welcome to Club Nitro!" Daniel told the crowd.

People clapped and cheered, including me. I quickly sat in the chair Daniel had left for me right next to the stage. I was thankful for his forethought. I felt much safer being right next to them.

"Thanks for the enthusiastic welcome. I'm Daniel and this is Willow," he said, "and together we are, *A*

*Fling of Strings.* We hope you all enjoy the show. Feel free to dance and sing along."

They opened their set with an upbeat cover that had the club hopping and people dancing. Daniel was playing his electric guitar and singing, with Willow accompanying him with her electric violin.

The clubbers seemed to be enjoying the music—with lots of people dancing on the makeshift dance floor. Willow and Daniel were playing their own music as well as popular covers that everyone enjoyed.

This club couldn't have been established for long. It seemed to be more thrown together last minute. Especially since it smelled of mold—underneath the cologne, perfume, and sweat that is.

There was something off about this club. Something that I didn't like. I couldn't really define what it was. But as the night progressed, there was a predatory vibe to the atmosphere that had me constantly looking over my shoulder.

While I listened to Willow and Daniel, I watched the crowd and tried to pinpoint the dark feeling.

Most of the people seemed normal, but what was normal? People hid behind veneers of normalcy all the time. Just like Ivan had hid behind a mask of stupidity. Any one of these people could be a rapists or a killer. And that's what scared me half to death.

I shouldn't have come. Sage and Alexei were right in telling me to stay home.

Willow and Daniel just finished the first half of their two hour set. They were taking a break and told the crowd they'd be back in thirty minutes.

Willow handed me a bottle of water when she sat down next to me. Daniel went off to the restroom.

"I brought extra. I knew they wouldn't let you bring your own in with you."

"Thanks. You guys sound so amazing together. It takes my breath away listening to you."

Willow smiled, "We feel the same way about watching you dance."

"This club is something else. Not exactly what I was expecting."

"Oh, honey, we didn't expect this kind of place either. The pay is good though. Most the clubbers in the bar area and on the dance floor seem fine. But there's something..."

"You feel it too? I wonder if there are less than legal things going on somewhere else?"

"I wouldn't be surprised. Daniel seems a little on edge too."

"I am on edge," Daniel said when he returned and heard Willow's statement, "We are within the general vicinity of Club M. This place has the same feel to it. Just less obvious."

"We'll finish our set, then we're out. You shouldn't have come," Daniel said looking at me. "But I shouldn't have asked you to. Sage is going to kill me."

"Stop. I'm an adult and can think for myself. But I agree. When you guys finish, we'll leave."

"I'll be right back. You guys stay here," Daniel said as he walked towards the makeshift bar.

I drank a bit of my water and watched as Daniel chatted with the guy at the bar. They had their heads very close together because it was extremely loud with the music playing and people talking.

I saw a girl at the end of the bar doing lines of what I assumed to be cocaine or something similar. It was illegal, whatever it happened to be. The drinking and drugs were blatant. How did they keep their doors open? Maybe that was why it seemed so thrown together.

The few waitstaff that I saw appeared drugged and wore a minimal amount of clothing—to the point that what clothing they did wear seemed more of an afterthought. Men and women were groping the staff as they delivered drinks.

We needed to leave.

I was so absorbed in people watching, that I almost missed Willow's admirer. He was standing directly behind her.

She was equally absorbed standing next to the stage chatting with a fan. When she realized someone was pressed to her backside, she stiffened. But before she was able to turn around, he leaned forward to whisper into her ear.

The change was dramatic. If I didn't know better, I'd say my wild Willow was blushing. The look on her face triggered a memory. That look reminded me of when she told me about her night at the art gallery. The same night I had been drugged and abducted.

She had participated in a living art exhibit hosted by the art gallery where she worked. It had been a private event in one of the larger back rooms.

Willow had to kneel on a pedestal—resting on her heels, with her hands behind her back—naked. At first I worried she had been forced, but she assured me that she had volunteered.

The event had lasted for over an hour and with her holding that position. When she thought she had heard the last of the patrons leave and was alone, she went to step off the pedestal. But then realized that there was a man standing right behind her.

*"I had no idea what he looked like. But damn—did he ever smell wonderful."*

She had closed her eyes and shrugged her shoulders—moaning a little to herself with the sweetest smile on her face. Just like right now. I remember thinking to myself—*it was funny how the heart and mind could conjure sensations and feelings from our senses. Pull them from our memories to live again.*

She'd told me how he'd overwhelmed her senses…

*"He stepped behind me and pressed against my naked back. I could feel the fine, soft weave of whatever he was wearing. A dove grey suit jacket, I later discovered. He gently pressed tight against me and leaned slightly to the right. He asked me what my name was. I told him. Then he asked my age. Twenty-five, I said. After that, things became interesting because he told me to call him Sir. I was not to speak unless asked a specific question. So I remained silent and waited. Anticipation bubbling in my veins. He had asked one final question. Was this my first time participating in the private rooms, as a living art exhibit, to which I replied—Yes, Sir."*

*"He said if I did as commanded, I would be rewarded. He backed that comment up with a soft, wet kiss to a spot right behind my ear. My stomach was quivering, like rest-*

*less butterflies about to take flight. From one simple kiss. A kiss that would have brought me to my knees, had I not been sitting on them already."*

Oh my God. That had been Trey. I looked at him and he just winked when he saw I had figured out the connection.

So much made sense now. Yet I still didn't understand the Riley connection—and there was one, that much was obvious. I'd just ask him, though not right now.

I felt safe now with Trey there. Though I knew he would tell Sage and soon. If he hadn't already.

Daniel was back and he and Willow were about to start the last half of their set. I turned just in time to see as Trey ran his hand along the right side of Willow's neck. Then gently gripped her long red hair to pull her head to the side—giving him better access to her neck.

I knew I should have looked away, but I was mesmerized. He placed a sucking kiss to the left side of her neck. I swear I heard Willow moan from where I stood. I looked away when Willow turned her head to receive his deep, penetrating kiss.

Geez, it was damned hot in here. I drank more water, laughing at myself and missing Sage.

I felt a tap on my shoulder and turned.

"He knows you're here," Trey said.

"I figured. As I explained to Alexei and Sage, I won't let Ivan rule my life."

"What would you say, if I told you that Ivan was in *this* club—right now?"

What were the fucking chances of that? I felt fear liquify my gut and accelerate my heart rate.

"Is he?"

A brief hesitation in Willow's violin pulled my attention to the stage.

Trey, Daniel, and I looked at Willow questioningly. She tipped her head in the direction past the bar, but kept playing. We followed her gaze. My eyes widened when I saw who stood there like a foul specter.

What in the hell?

Turning my attention back to the stage, Daniel and Willow quickly ended their song.

And the haunting tune of Hozier's "Take Me To Church" began.

# CHAPTER TWENTY-EIGHT

# Daniel

There was no plausible explanation as for why my father, the esteemed Quinton Daniel Creighton would be at this particular club in LA. The club where I happened to be playing. Doing the very thing that he abhorred.

By the look on his face, good old dad was as equally surprised to see me. But just as quickly, his face morphed back into its usual scowl of displeasure and disappointment.

Willow and I had been playing the club circuit for over a month now—finally pursuing our passion for music. It had been the right thing to do and was completely liberating for the both of us.

Willow was thriving and completely in her element. She had been more than ready to make a change she had told me.

*"I need to shake my life up a bit. I've been bored senseless and tired of my moping ways. I miss Ava."* She'd confessed, with a mixture of sadness and determination resonating in her eyes.

When I asked her about why she was so upset, she had said, *"Let's just say, that my love life is so anemic right now, that I might need a transfusion just to raise it from nonexistent to barely above pathetic.*"

When I shook my head in confusion and questioned her, "*But I thought...*"

She cut me off and refused to talk about it. We still hadn't discussed the subject again, but she seemed happy now.

We loved the music scene that we were creating for ourselves. Willow was extremely talented. Not only did she play the violin, but she played the piano too. She sang quite beautifully, but would only sing with me if I had bribed or dared her into doing so.

Keeping all of this a secret from Mason was weighing heavily on my mind. So my current happiness was tinged with remorse. The next time he came home during his bye week, I would have to sit him down and confess to all that had been going on.

That was not a conversation I was looking forward to—on multiple levels.

But now I was faced with a more pressing problem— my father.

I quickly changed the song and jumped directly into another. Willow caught on straight away and fell in sync.

The song was quite fitting. As we played, I astutely ignored my father's hateful presence.

As I sang, memories from my childhood surfaced. Especially one. A pivotal memory—etched upon me and in multiple ways...

*Music had always been the passion of my soul, not that I had been allowed to pursue it within the confines of our rigid household. The piano would have been an acceptable choice in my father's eyes, but only if I played classical music upon the black and white's.*

*When I'd been about ten years old, I distinctly remember staying the night at my friend Jimmy's house. He had a guitar and had been taking lessons. So Jimmy had showed me how to play a few chords. I picked up his guitar and tried it for myself. Though I had never played before, it had come naturally.*

*I was transformed in that moment and of course had dreams of being a huge rock star. The next day I begged my mother to buy a guitar for me. She had. I'd been too excited and only ten at the time to realize how out of character that had been for her. It was the last spontaneous thing she had ever done for me.*

*I knew well enough to hide my guitar in the closet and only play it when my father wasn't home. He would have never approved. He'd been away at trial that night and not expected home until later in the evening. I'd felt safe to grab my acoustic guitar and let my fingers fly. I'd loved to play along with the radio—rearranging popular songs.*

*That night I'd been so absorbed in the music that I hadn't heard the front door slam shut—announcing my father's early arrival home. A continuance had been granted to the opposition, so court had finished earlier than expected, allowing him to come home early. Unfortunately, he heard me playing my guitar—my secret.*

*The bedroom door had opened with cold deliberation—silent upon its hinges. I had seen my father enter my room from the corner of my frightened eyes. He'd walked over to me and held out his hand—no words were spoken, or necessary.*

*The pain I felt in that moment, as I'd handed him my guitar, would resonate through my entire life.*

Though I wouldn't recognize the impact of that event until now...

*I followed him from what had then been my sanctuary, my safe haven, to the back yard.*

*He waited until I had been standing before him and attentive to his every gesture. As if I could have missed a thing, as my eyes were wide and pleading—though solemn with acceptance. He'd stared at me without emotion, making sure he had my undivided attention.*

*I followed the progress of my guitar, still held in his hand, as he'd raised it high above his head. I'd known what was coming and watched helplessly as he had opened his hand and let it go.*

*My guitar had dropped rapidly to land on the stone pavers below our feet. Fracturing through the body.*

*My father had not been satisfied with those results. Oh no.*

*In retrospect, I'm sure he assumed it would shatter at his feet and when it didn't he took exacting measures to rectify the situation. He would make sure that it was well and truly destroyed. Along with my defiance.*

*He had used his foot next to ensure that it was properly done.*

The discordant sound echoed through me still. To this day I wore the evidence of his disappointment under my right eye—where a piece of the splintered guitar had cut me. That cut was the least of the damage that had been done that fateful day, but it was the only injury that had ever been visible. I can still recall my father methodically straightening his clothes after he'd finished with his destruction of my guitar...

*A clump of hair had fallen across his forehead, he swiped angrily at it by shoving his hand through his hair to fix that one errant lock. I didn't move or change my position until my father had left to go back inside. And then I still waited.*

*I looked back towards the house. When I was sure all was clear, I slowly gathered the remnants of my guitar. I'd taken all of it to the trash can on the side of the house. He would expect it of me and would check.*

*As I passed by my parents' window, I heard a noise coming from inside their room. I stopped, afraid to move. It had sounded much like when I'm playing football and get the wind knocked out of me from a tackle. But that made no sense, until I heard my mother cry out.*

*Did he hit her? Naw, he wouldn't have done that. But I couldn't imagine why she would cry out.*

Leaning over my Martin, I played Hozier's "Take Me To Church"—allowing my fingers and Willow's violin to eloquently speak my message. My mind drifted to the memory of when Mason first gave my guitar to me...

*We had been hanging out at his house, as we rarely hung out at mine—too many rules. It had been several months since the destruction of my guitar. I'd not spoken about it with Mason. How do you tell your best friend something like that. I'd kept it all to myself, but somehow Mason had known something had happened to it.*

*"Daniel, will you go to my room and get my football? I'll get us some water and we can meet out back and throw the ball around. Oh and Ava is coming by after ballet practice. I'll grab some snacks too," Mason yelled over his shoulder, laughing on his way to the kitchen.*

*I laughed too, because for such a petite girl Ava had always been hungry and eating. She was tall, but delicate from her years of ballet. She and I were about the same height, but geez I hoped that changed soon.*

*We were all ten years old and had been best friends forever. I'd walked into Mason's room and there laying on the bed had been the Martin. Of course back then I had no clue it was a Martin. I only knew that there was a guitar lying on my best friend's bed, but I wasn't at all jealous because I knew it was for me.*

*I'd picked it up and turned around to sit on the bed, the football forgotten as I'd began strumming. I'd ignored the childish tears that had gathered in my eyes to blur my vision and had played by feel, as they'd dripped onto the neck of the guitar. I heard a noise by the door and had looked up to see Mason watching me play, his hands tucked into the back pockets of his Levis. Good friend that he was, Mason had ignored the tears that had dripped off my chin.*

*"Are you coming or what? Ava is outside eating all the snacks." Mason said, as he'd turned and left to go outside.*

*"I'm coming," I'd replied hoarsely to his retreating back. I scooped up the football and the guitar.*

Pulled from my memories, I looked up and saw my father walking away.

"What the fuck?" I mouthed to Willow and Ava.

# CHAPTER TWENTY-NINE

# Sage

After our conversation on Wednesday, Lieut. Clarke sent officers to watch the shipping yard. They tailed every eighteen wheeler that left. Tedious, but it paid off last night.

Late Thursday night and into the early morning hours of Friday, we met with our hand-selected group of detectives and officers. We knew these officers were clean and could be trusted. We didn't want Peacock or his cronies tipped off as to what we were about to throw down.

We had a search warrant and all the necessary legalities were buttoned up. There would be no questions and no loopholes for their lawyers to bail them out.

Based on the conversation I overheard at the bar on Tuesday, we suspected the traffickers would be transporting their kidnapped victims across state lines—on Friday. But we weren't waiting for that to occur. We would shut down this local tributary of the human trafficking scene. And reunite some of these lost souls with their families.

At our meeting, we strategized how best to approach the hotel. After assessing the building plans, we divvied up the team into four groups. Each team was assigned to an access point.

There was a double-doored main entrance at the center of the hotel on the frontside, exit doors on either end of the hotel, and a single-doored exit on the backside of the hotel. There were no balconies or terraces to the individual hotel rooms.

When Friday evening arrived, we met down the street from the hotel. It was located in a commercially depressed, out-of-the-way area, between LA and Pasadena.

Before the economy had slid into a recession, this area had been thriving with local businesses. But, post-recession, the local industry had dried up and the hotel was abandoned for not turning a profit.So it was the perfect set up and just what these human traffickers were looking for.

Purchased on the cheap, they could implement inexpensive modifications. This would give them the perfect place to house and run their flesh peddling businesses.

Unlike the original hotel owners though, they had no trouble turning a profit. Illegal gains made from the kidnapped men and women pressed into prostitution or sold on the black market. Lost souls kept compliant through drugs, coercion, both physical and mental abuse, take your pick—they implemented them all.

And these fuckers were hiding in plain sight. Right here in the good ole USA.

In my own backyard.

The prominently displayed *no vacancy* sign seemed out of place for this type of hotel. But it got the job done. The hotel looked completely occupied, especially with the amount of cars that came and went on a regular basis.

The traffickers knew what they were doing. It was big money and it paid to be smart. They formed clubs of men and women who would have exclusive access to these hotels and sex clubs. There was a message system controlled by the traffickers to let the club members know about new locations.

I had just passed that vetting process, when I was undercover a few months ago. Ivan had taken me to Club M, one of his more exclusive clubs. It had been my entry into the dark world of human trafficking. But it had all gone to hell when Ivan had shot me—rescuing Ava from his imprisonment.

In the Dark folder, Brent had mentioned the dark web. It must be similar to the deep web I had accessed to read the Dark folder. He mentioned that when you were in the dark web that anything and everything could be bought and sold there. It made sense to use, as it was private. Untraceable and accessible from anywhere with internet access.

Lieut. Clarke actually knew more than I did about the deep web and the dark web. I believed that the secret group Brent alluded to operated within the deep web. I wasn't positive, but I planned to find out.

I knew that Ivan had to be involved with this hotel, and with this group of traffickers, and we were looking for ways to connect him.

I wanted him found. I wanted his blood. He needed him to pay.

There was an eighteen wheeler parked on the backside of the hotel. The side loading door was hidden from view. We suspected they would load the truck with everyone who was being transported to Mexico and the black market. By what Peacock implied, they would be cleaning house tonight.

We decided it would be safer to wait until the truck was fully loaded and the hotel vacated. No collateral damage that way and no innocents hurt in the potential crossfire.

I felt my iPhone watch vibrate with a text message.
*At club Nitro*
*Ava's here*
*So is Ivan*
Fuck!

I knew Trey would keep her safe. I put my worry aside and focused on the here and now.

We heard gunfire coming from inside.

Double Fuck!

We'd been on radio silence, as we were all well versed in our roles.

But this was a game changer.

"Report."

"Definite gunfire."

"Go time. Take out the hostels at the truck."

"On it."

The guards by the truck had heard the gunfire too. A few of them ran inside—leaving minimal support outside.

"We're clear at the truck."

We watched the truck drive off with our man at the wheel. They were headed to a local hospital. They were set up and ready for the influx of multiple victims.

The hotel was four stories. Each team had a floor to sweep. I was sweeping the second floor. Once the truck drove off and with the catalyst of the gunfire—the electricity was cut.

Hoping the hostiles were blind, we went in with our night vision activated.

A back-up generator kicked on, but provided minimal light.

The stairwell was clear. Our team had split and half went up the North stairwell and the other half the South. There were eighteen rooms on each floor, so it shouldn't take too long to search.

My team heard something a few doors down on our right. The goons were suspiciously quiet.

The low profile door-frames made protecting our bodies difficult. Thank God for combat gear.

"I'm not sorry. You're fucking pigs!" A young woman yelled.

Signaling to the team—we moved forward.

"Thought you could fuck me one more time. Didn't you? Your little *blayd*."

Another shot rang out followed by a grunt of pain. I flinched in memory.

"Fuck me, then send me off to be sold! To some unknown asshole!"

We inched along the wall. I signaled the team I was going put eyes on the situation.

"Fuck that! And fuck you!"

I looked through the crack created between the opened door and the frame...

"My name isn't, *blayd*. It's Jade! Do you hear me? Jade!"

And shook my head—shocked at what I saw.

# Ivan

"What the fuck are you playing at, Ivan? Why is Daniel here?" Quinton Creighton, my attorney, demanded after barging into my office.

Jesus, now what? Things were going to shit at Hotel Dark. I had no time and zero patience.

"Quinton. Come in, won't you."

"Don't take that patronizing tone with me. You may be the leader of the LA Dark, but I'm the Dark's legal counsel for this region."

"What do you want? You have eyes and ears. Your son is playing the guitar and singing."

"Why here? Why would you bring him into one of our clubs? What are you trying to pull?"

"I have more important things to deal with right now. You can leave. Your whining has grown tiresome."

"You're deluded if you believe the Supremacy and the Elders aren't aware of what you've been doing. Regardless if they are aware now or not, they will be—because I plan to tell them. You are recklessly exposing them."

"Threats?" I stood and slowly slipped my hands into my pockets. Walking around to the other side of the desk, I rested back against the edge.

"You're in no position to threaten me. You would do well to remember your place."

"My place, as you so succinctly put it, is to protect the interests of the Dark—not yours. They have no desire to be discovered. In case you've forgotten,secrecy is their aim. Yet, you flaunt their ideals with little regard."

"Do you remember that I brought you into this organization, Quinton? When you were nothing? Do you?" My anger was escalating. "I think that you might be in need of another lesson—on your knees. That can be arranged."

"That won't happen again—ever." His eyes darted to the door, betraying his fear.

"I beg to differ. Yosef?" I called out to my right hand man. He stepped into the office from where he had been hidden around the corner.

"Sir."

"I'm thinking that the good Quinton here is in need of another lesson in the Dark's hierarchy. What think you?"

"That can be arranged, Sir. Now?" Yosef asked, though more for show than for enquiry. He knew what my desires would be.

"Now, Yosef."

Within moments Yosef had him kneeling before me. The look of fear on his face was the sweetest aphrodisiac. When he would have stood, Yosef nailed him hard with a swift kick to his left kidney. His grunt of pain was music to my ears. I savored the scent of fear rolling off him in waves.

"Now, where were we? You were threatening to have a chat with the Supremacy and the Elders. Do you really think they'd believe you? Over me? Now I ask you, who is the deluded one?"

"They're on to you. Mark my words, Ivan." Quinton's voice cracked on his empty threats and rising fear. His pathetic attempt to appear in a position of power, while kneeling before me.

"You've fucked up this time. It won't be me, Ivan. You're the one who'll be taught a lesson. I..."

"There are no lessons to be taught here after all," I said as I'd pulled my combat knife out of pocket, gripped it in my fist, and pulled the blade hard across his neck—cutting him off mid-sentence, pun intended, I chuckled to myself.

"Well, that's unfortunate. Now we'll have to find another attorney," I said to Yosef, as he brought me a drink, "Shouldn't be too difficult."

"Cheers, old friend," I said and raised my glass in the air.

Tonight was not going according to plan. Every time I turned around, I was rudely interrupted. First Hotel Dark, then my dead lawyer. What's next, I thought angrily and tossed back my drink.

I would just have to comfort myself with my plans for Ava. Her imminent sacrifice and death soothed the beast stirring in my mind.

# Scar

There was thinking that you knew something and then *really* knowing it. So seeing the first-hand evidence of Ivan's evil was quite another thing altogether.

She couldn't believe what she had just witnessed. Yet she wasn't surprised at all. Ivan had just nonchalantly killed his attorney, Quinton Creighton. She knew that he was just as evil as Ivan—so he'd deserved it and in spades.

Besides most corporate attorneys were soulless, career driven narcissists—she should know.

Ivan's man, Yosef, was there and had helped Ivan with the killing of his attorney. She'd seen it all go down from where she'd been hiding in a tiny closet.

She had been waiting for the right time to present herself to Ivan. When she would have left the sanctuary of that closet, Yosef had come into the office. But he quickly hid in an alcove directly in front of her hiding space when Quinton had stormed in.

She held her breath thinking all would be lost and she would be discovered before her careful plans could be implemented.

It had taken her years of sacrifice, pain, and deep undercover work—some of which had destroyed what was left of her soul, to finally arrive at this moment. Would she savor that moment, gloating and degrading his life once she took it?

Like he had—just now?

She was afraid to know the answer to that. Afraid that in actuality, she was no better than he was. Though she felt she had righteousness on her side of the equation to balance the scales in her favor. Or so she hoped.

She would forfeit whatever price there was to pay to see him dead. She would see this done, once and for all, no matter the cost.

Before Yosef had come in, she'd heard Ivan having a heated conversation on his phone. Evidently LAPD had just raided one of his trafficking hotels when a shipment was being loaded for delivery.

Good, she thought. Hopefully that would put a huge dent in his operations—though she doubted it.

"Yosef," Ivan said before taking a swallow of his drink, "LAPD raided Hotel Dark."

"Yes, I had just heard that when I'd come in. I was going to discuss this with you before we were so rudely interrupted," Yosef replied, before giving Quinton's dead body a swift kick for emphasis.

"Did you also hear who was leading the way? One of the guards saw him outside afterwards," Ivan asked.

"Sage Cartier. Yes, that was also mentioned."

Her eyes widened at Sage's name, though she wasn't surprised. She had been notified when he accessed the Dark folder via the deep web. And he wasn't the kind of detective that would sit on information.

"He has become a problem that needs to be dealt with. But I will do it. Tell the men that he's off limits. He's mine."

"Yes, Sir."

"He's ruining all my hard work. Like a fucking roach, he keeps popping up and fucking with my operations."

Ivan's Russian accent had thickened with his anger.

"He took Ava from me. My men told me they overheard he proposed to her. I'll take her back tonight. She will be my best sacrifice yet! Did you see her sitting by the stage?"

"I did."

Sage was engaged to this Ava? She was shocked to say the least. He needed to know that Ivan intended on killing her.

"Then he had someone steal Lilly from me at Club M. She was my best greeter. Her father still needs to pay for that. Remind me later so that I don't forget."

"Yes, Sir. Have you spoken with the Supremacy or the Elders lately?" Yosef asked.

Scar didn't know who that was. Those names had never surfaced during her investigations.

"No, I've been very busy organizing this shipment of stock for my client in Mexico. He wanted everything from Hotel Dark and from Kansas City, as you well know."

"The Supremacy wanted me to deliver a personal message from him to you. He wanted it hand delivered and conveyed as much, stating that he felt it would be the only acceptable method of delivery."

"Oh, I'm listening," Ivan had said with a condescending tone ripe with impatience.

It was obvious that he felt that the Supremacy, whoever that was, should have given him the personal message directly.

"Would you like another drink?" Yosef asked, instead of giving Ivan the message.

"No, I wouldn't. What I would like, Yosef, is for you to give me the message the Supremacy told you to deliver. You should have given it to me when you received it. Making me wait is unacceptable."

"As you wish," Yosef said as he put his drink down.

She could barely see what was going on through the minuscule crack in the door. But she watched as Yosef walked over to where Ivan was standing and placed his hands on Ivan's shoulders while facing him.

Yosef wasn't a bad looking guy—superficially—she thought. He was probably six feet tall and had a slim, yet athletic build. He had a square jaw, short dark hair and eyes, and was impeccably dressed in a European suit.

"In honor of the Supremacy's position, as leader of the Dark, and following his explicit wishes, I do faithfully discharge my duties," Yosef said formally.

Scar slowly sank to the floor of the small closet when she heard the message delivered by Yosef.

# CHAPTER THIRTY-TWO

# Sage

I shook my head when the young woman saw me through the crack. I gave her a huge amount of credit for not giving me away to the men in the room. She had one of their guns and pointed it at the two men on the floor. Another was on the ground near the bed. Not moving. Dead, I hoped.

"You will say my name. Now! Or I will fucking kill you too!" She continued, not missing a beat.

The two fucktards on the ground were in no position to do anything but comply. They were looking up at the business end of their own gun—they'd best say her name and quick.

"Jade," they said in unison.

I gave Jade a head jerk towards the corner of the room, when she looked my way. I wanted her to move away from the entrance. Put distance between herself and the guys on the floor.

She kept the gun steady, bracing it with both of her hands and stepped backwards a few feet, saying, "You're lucky you said it. I wouldn't have hesitated to shoot you —again."

"As soon my men are here, *Jade,* I will make you pay for that." One of the idiots on the ground threatened.

That's when we made our move. Rushing the room and incapacitating the hostiles.

"I don't think so," I said and *tripped* my way into the room. My fist landing in his face as I fell into him. Once they were restrained, my men took them away.

"Nice work, Jade. Those fucktards had no idea that we were here." I kept my tone light including her in our ranks.

I looked around the room. The conditions she'd been kept in were deplorable. There were no other hostiles—dead or alive.

Wanting to cover her emaciated and abused body, I searched the room for something for her to wear. But there was nothing except the dirty sheets on the bed, and fuck if I would wrap those nasty things around her.

She wore her courage like a robe and seemed unconcerned over her nakedness.

Her blonde hair was wild and her green eyes were wide and dilated—bruised and haunted.

I unbuckled my kevlar vest and a few eyebrows kicked up. I handed the vest to the detective on my left.

We still hadn't taken her gun. We needed to and we would. But for now, she needed to feel like she was in control.

"Here, let me hold your gun, so you can put this on." Pulling my t-shirt off, I handed it to Jade. "I'll give it back to you. Promise."

She stared at me unmoving. Weighing her options. Debating.

Trust was a fragile commodity.

Nodding her head at me she said, "Thank you. I...I'm not feeling so good." Jade was swaying on her feet.

Post-adrenaline rush and subsequent crash. I reached out and took the gun as she handed it to me. And then, I gave it to the detective.

"Here, let me help you put the shirt on," I said, then proceeded to pull it over her head and put her arms through. My jaw clenched at the evidence of her abuse.

Her pale skin was covered in bruises.

"Do you want the gun back? You can have it."

"No, I don't even like guns. I've never shot one before."

Looking up at me, she asked in a whisper, "Is he dead?"

I turned to the detective who had been attending him. He nodded.

"Yes, Jade, he's dead."

"Good, he fucking deserved it."

I didn't respond to that, because I had no doubt that he did.

She turned away and said, "He was the worst."

The quiet, shattered statement tore through me. Here was my Ava, all over again.

"Can you tell what day it is?" She asked.

"It's Friday."

She nodded, "but—what month? What year?" She asked, but didn't give me time to answer before continuing, "I've been here for over one hundred and eighty-one days now. That's how many lines I put in that stupid closet."

She walked to the closet and opened the door to illustrate her point. Inside and scored upon the back wall was row upon row of lines marching out her time spent here in purgatory. There were too many to count with just a brief glance.

"Jade? Do you remember when you were taken?"

"It was about six months ago—in September. I was drugged a lot in the beginning."

I couldn't tell her it had been over a year ago.

"An ambulance is here to take you to the hospital. I'm going to have them to take you to Cedars-Sinai. There is a doctor there that I want you to work with, her name is Dr. Wong. She and her nurse, Audrey, will take good care of you, Jade."

"No. No, I just want to go home to my family," she said, with a quiet desperation, but with steel threaded through her voice.

"You're scared. You're hurt. But you're strong, Jade."

My men told me in my earpiece that the ambulance was there.

"You defended yourself. You're free."

My watch was alerting me again that Trey was texting me. Fuck!

"Dr. Wong helped my fiancée," I told her simply.

She looked at me questioningly. I nodded slightly, as if to say, yes, for the same reason.

"Okay. I'll go. Thank you?"

"Detective Sage Cartier."

"Thank you, Detective."

"There will be a lot questions, Jade. And an exam. Is your family here? In California?"

She shook her head no. "It will take them a while to get here. But I'll call them later. After all that hospital business is done."

"How did you arrive here?"

"At Hotel Dark? Some douchebag named Marcus. He invited me out for drinks with some dancer friends. They all seemed so harmless. Ballet dancers? I would have never thought they'd drug me. But they did."

"He's dead. Marcus that is. If that helps."

"It does. I don't recognize who I am anymore. I think Jade died, and I'm someone else."

"Dr. Wong and Audrey will help you."

My watch was buzzing again. Trey.

"Jade, do you have anything you want to bring with you? The ambulance is here now."

She looked around the room.

"No," she said with a shake of her head, "The precious items that I arrived with were stolen long ago. And there are no replacements."

She walked out of that hell hole with her head held high.

We protected her on the way out, just in case. I pulled up the rear and one of the other officers protected her front.

My watch and phone buzzed constantly.

Something bad must have happened—just how bad, was what had me worried.

# CHAPTER THIRTY-THREE

# Scar

Yosef still had his hands on Ivan's shoulders when he began to deliver the message.

"I won't bore you with all the details, Sir."

She heard the sarcasm in his voice when he said, "Sir," but did Ivan she wondered?

"I've taken the liberty to paraphrase the message for you. The Supremacy wanted to be sure that there were no misunderstandings."

"Yosef, your belaboring of this point is grating on my nerves. Deliver the message already."

"As you wish. But I'd like to quote you first, Ivan, because it suits the message perfectly."

"Where, Ivan, is *your* deserve it factor?"

He still had ahold of Ivan's shoulders and Ivan was looking at him blanking. She was equally confused.

"Too greedy, Ivan. Too careless, too greedy, and too stupid—to live."

With that final statement, Yosef hand delivered the Supremacy's message to the very wide-eyed Ivan.

Between one breath and the next, Yosef grabbed Ivan by the head and twisted quickly, breaking his neck.

Yosef let go and Ivan crumpled to the ground—dead.

She put her hand to her mouth and bit down to keep from yelling out. Tears of frustration and pain breaching her control to fall unheeded down her cheeks.

Now what would she do? Her plans—ruined.

But the horror-fest continued.

Yosef pulled out his cell phone and a pack of cigarettes. He lit one, taking a long drag and exhaling on a sigh.

"It's Yosef. Your message has been delivered and dispatched. Yes, he was surprised," he said, taking another drag of his cigarette and nodded his head, "I have the program ready. It will wipe the hard drive and the fire will take care of the rest. As you wish, Maxim."

He walked over and picked up a water bottle that had been sitting by her closet hell. He poured the liquid around the room, dousing everything, including the two dead bodies.

He grabbed some files out of the desk and inserted a flash drive into the USB port of the laptop. He hit a couple keys on the keyboard—and that was that. He threw his cigarette into the far corner, turned, and walked out.

She could read the writing on the wall and it spelled crispy-critter, as the liquid he had poured everywhere caught fire.

She flew out of the closet and right to the computer. She wanted the information on that hard drive. Pulling the flash drive out, she threw it. Though it was probably too late to save the hard drive from being wiped clean, she had to try. She shoved the Mac laptop into her satchel.

Heat and smoke were consuming the room—making it difficult to breathe. Taking the plant off the desk, she smashed it onto the floor and the line of accelerant hoping to buy herself some time.

Looking at Ivan one last time, she turned and ran from the room. But when she tried to open the door, the knob turned, so it wasn't locked, but it wouldn't budge.

Screaming in frustration, she kicked at the door—hard and fast with her foot.

Grabbing the handle, she pulled hard and stumbled backwards as the door suddenly gave way. A rush of fresh air flooded the room and she ran as fast as she could through the door and down the corridor.

She turned back to see a momentary pause in the fire. Then there was a sudden flash, as an explosion of heat, smoke and fire erupted. The smoke chased her down the hallway with the fire close behind and consuming the old building as it went.

The smoke had preceded her to the club floor where all was in chaos. No fire system had been activated. No water, no alarms—nothing. Hopefully it was just delayed and not absent. The fire was getting closer and she could feel the heat.

She saw people on their phones. Help would be on the way. But these people needed to leave and now.

"Move it people!" She yelled at the clubbers, hoping to be heard above the chaos. It was futile.

She was running out to the rooftop when she saw Daniel, Quinton's son, run past her.

He was going in the wrong direction. Towards the smoke and fire of the backrooms instead of away.

Crazy-ass kid!

She kept going. If he wanted to die with his evil father—so be it. Forgetting about him, she ran out the club doors and onto the rooftop deck—aiming for the fire escape.

It was chaos here too.

Some club guy had stepped forward to help organize the masses. He was herding them towards the fire escape to get them off the roof and away from the building. A shocking display of heroics in an era of proliferate selfishness.

Shamed, she turned around and ran back towards the smoke—and Daniel.

# CHAPTER THIRTY-FOUR

# Ava

The club went from drinking and dancing to utter chaos when smoke and fire came funneling down the hallway. Clubbers were running around chaotically and the staff took the opportunity to bail.

Everyone was in self-preservation mode—and it was complete pandemonium!

"Daniel, come back!" I screamed, as he took off running towards the worst of the smoke.

"Get to safety! I'm going to find my father," he yelled back to us, as he ran past a redhead coming from that direction.

I saw her look towards Daniel in recognition, shake her head, and continue running towards the rooftop deck—coughing as she went.

Willow and I were left alone amidst the craziness.

"He'll come back. Let's go," I yelled to Willow.

"Grab Daniel's acoustic guitar!" she said, as she grabbed her beloved violin.

We ran towards the rooftop deck that was just outside the club doors. We saw Trey on the other side of the room as we were running out. He was yelling our names and coming towards us, but when saw we were on our way out, he changed his direction to meet us there.

"I saw Daniel take off towards the back. Where in the hell is he going?" Trey asked when we met up outside.

"He took off after his asshole of a father," Willow answered, then coughed from the smoke.

"Come here," Trey demanded, before he pulled Willow into his arms and kissed her soundly.

I looked away to give them a private moment—among the hundreds of people—but they broke away after mere seconds.

"I called 911, as did others. Firetrucks are on their way. But we are leaving now. We need to get off this building and away from the fire," Trey said wielding his authority and dominance.

Assuring our compliance, Trey gently grabbed our arms and started walking quickly towards the corner of the rooftop. The fire escape was located there and so was the long line to climb down.

"Have you seen Ivan?" Trey asked.

My throat felt raw and my eyes were stinging. I started coughing before I could respond and settled for shaking my head in the negative.

"He's here. Somewhere," Trey said, scanning the area, which was packed with frantic people.

"I won't give him the opportunity to make a grab for you in the chaos, Ava. So we're leaving—now."

I kept searching for Daniel, but I didn't see him anywhere. There were so many people and with the smoke that was coming from the doors made visibility difficult.

I wanted him to come back before we had to go down the stairs. He would understand. I wouldn't have to say a thing. Fire or falling to my death, neither prospect sounded great.

Fear was all but choking me.

Trey kept a firm grip on my arm and Willow's, so that we wouldn't get separated in the mass of people. The closer we got to the front of the line, the sicker I became.

One of the clubbers had stepped forward to calm people down and organize the evacuation chaos.

"Down the fire escape, ladies. Let's go!" Trey said, when our turn came.

Trey went first. That way, he explained, Willow and I would be above him. Just in case we lost our grip.

That would work perfectly for my plans of staying right where I was.

I took out my phone and sent a quick text to my father and then to Sage. Stating simply...

*I love you.*

Nothing more was needed. I didn't want to worry them or confess to the danger that I was in. There was nothing they could do in any case.

Trey stepped up first on to the low three foot wall and grabbed the railing to the fire escape. Daniel's guitar hung over his back. He turned around and took several steps down. He looked to Willow and I to go next.

"Go, Willow. You go first. I'll be right behind you. Hurry, Trey is waiting. He's holding up the line. God, he's stubborn and demanding."

"You have no idea," Willow said with a look that I didn't quite understand and was too distracted to figure out.

Willow stepped up onto the ledge and grabbed the handles to the fire escape. Mimicking the exact movements Trey had taken.

Turning around, she stood in the cradle of Trey's arms. Her violin hanging safely in front of her. As they started to descend down the stairs, they both looked up at me.

I still hadn't stepped forward to take my turn.

"Come on, Ava. Let's go!" Willow implored.

I shook my head and stepped slightly out of line.

Willow and Trey had no choice but to descend. Trey did not look too happy with me. But he didn't understand my fear. There was no way I could make myself go over that edge.

The line was pressing forward.

I was being crowded from behind and pushed towards the fire escape.

Behind me, a drunk girl was slurring profanities at me.

"Hurry the fuck up or move the fuck out of the way, bitch. You may wanna fry your skinny ass, but I want off this roof. Now!" she said, as she impatiently pushed her way past me.

Her unexpected shove caused me to lose my balance. *How could I be graceful on stage, but not in everyday life?* I thought as I stumbled towards the edge of the building.

And fell over the rooftop wall.

# CHAPTER THIRTY-FIVE

# Sage

Once Jade was in the ambulance and on her way to the hospital, I grabbed my phone out of my pocket and saw there was a message from Ava.

*I love you*

That was it. That's all she wrote. Something was wrong, I knew she was in danger, I could feel it.

I reached out to Trey—he'd been phoning non-stop.

"There was a fire at the club," Trey said in greeting, "Willow and I made it down the fire escape, but Ava refused to come down."

"Fuck!"

"That about sums it up."

"I'm on my way."

As I ran to my car, I yelled to one of the detectives that I was heading downtown. They could wrap this up just as easily as I could.

"Update Lieut. Clarke," I instructed.

"I'm going back up now," Trey was telling me, "I had to wait until everyone came down. One-way traffic and all."

"Is she in danger? What's the status of LAFD?" I asked, as I jumped into the rental and took off.

"The sprinklers came on, but it's an old building. I'd feel better, as I'm sure you would, if she were on the ground."

"I'm calling her now."

As I waited for Ava to pick up her phone, I sent her a quick text too.

*I love you too*

*I'm on my way*

*Please stay safe*

Come on, Beauty. Pick up!

*"Hi, this is Ava. Please leave a message and I'll get back to you."* She giggled before continuing, *"If I can stop myself from dancing, that is."*

I gripped the steering wheel tight with my abraded left hand and flew across town. My hand ached from hitting that asshole at Hotel Dark. I should have pummeled his face until it had been properly rearranged. Maybe I was no better than he was, but I'd do it—just to avenge those helpless women he had abused over the years.

When the *beep* sounded, I left a message that mirrored the texted one, but I wanted her to hear my voice. Hear how much I loved her and was worried for her safety. I should have looked at my watch or my phone when Trey had first started contacting me.

If something happens to her because I ignored those messages...

# CHAPTER THIRTY-SIX

# Ava

Paralyzed, I hung over the edge—looking straight down.

Twenty stories to the street below.

Vertigo assailed me. My vision blurred and the world began spinning out of control.

Fear seized my lungs and breathing became impossible.

Dancing spots flirted with my waning vision and the edges darkened, tunneling into a pin point of light.

Oh, God! This is it.

*What goes up, must come down.*

Gravity, that bitch, always wins. I thought inanely, as I slipped further. The old bricks ripped at my skin until I finally came to rest against my armpit—my legs useless under me.

"Whoa there, girl! Come back onto this side of the wall before you fall to your death." Some guy said, as he picked me up off the wall and set me onto my feet.

Luckily he still had ahold of my arms or I would have crumbled where I stood.

"I know there's a lot of smoke and fire, but the sprinklers are on and things are less grim than they were." My savior, which also happened to be the same guy organizing the evacuation, told me. "So there's no need to jump off the roof. You should have plenty of time to go down the slo-mo way—via the fire escape," he finished, emphasizing that last part.

Wide-eyed in terror and mouth dried of all moisture, I bobbled my head in response.

I pointed to the far corner of the roof, which was far away from the edge and the smoke.

He helped to get me over there, knowing that I was in no shape to attempt the fire escape just then without falling to my death in truth.

I sat down with my back to the wall and took shallow breaths. I hugged my knees to my chest and tried to calm my racing heart and rebelling stomach.

I should probably just vomit and be done with it. Ugh, I hated to throw up!

Deep breath Ava, deep breath.

I had no plans beyond sitting here and hoping to survive the smoke and the fire. The fire department should be here any minute. I'd wait to make any decisions until I absolutely had to.

I didn't think I could make myself go over that ledge again, not even if I was upright and walking on my own two feet, instead of hanging over the edge.

Now that my adrenaline had completely hit rock bottom and its anesthetizing affect had worn off—my arm felt like it was on fire. I saw that deep gouges had been ripped into the soft skin on the underside of my bicep and forearm.

Slow and steady blood dripped onto my jeans.

Pulling off the multicolored sash that I had worn with my jeans tonight, I wound it tight around my arm. I looked up when I finished to see that the line to get off the roof was all but gone now.

I could still feel the heat of the fire from where I sat in the far corner. I was all but alone now—waiting.

The sound of coughing drew my attention towards the exit of the club.

Just beyond the club doors, where smoke still poured out, was the redhead I had seen earlier. She was bent over with her hands on her knees and coughing uncontrollably. Near her feet, lay a person who was also coughing, just not as forcefully. More like a wheeze.

I jumped up to go offer my assistance and stumbled into the wall, listing as if drunk. I dropped down to a squat and waited for the world to stop spinning.

This time I stood up slowly and made my way to-wards the redhead on shaky legs. At least I didn't feel like I was going to pass out this time.

She looked up at me as I approached. Her skin was red, as if sunburned, and the hair around her face was singed in places. I cried out when I saw that it was Daniel laying on the ground beneath her.

I grabbed a discarded water bottle on my way there and handed it to her. She looked at it thoughtfully for a second, shrugged her shoulders, and poured some into her mouth. Then on her face.

"Daniel?" I yelled unnecessarily loud. I looked him over from head to toe. He seemed to be okay—a little singed like the redhead. His eyes were closed and he had that wheezing quality to his breathing.

I looked at the redhead and asked, "could you help me move him? To that corner," I pointed to where I had been sitting, "it's shielded from the smoke. It might help."

Instead of answering me, she stuck the water bottle in her back pocket, and grabbed him under his armpits. I grabbed his feet and together we carried him over to the corner.

Once in the corner, I let go of his feet and ran around the redhead. I quickly sat cross-legged on the ground. She laid him down and his head was resting on my lap.

Red handed me the water bottle and I poured a little into my hands and wiped it over Daniel's face. The fresh air was having the desired effect and he seemed to be breathing a little easier, though still wheezing.

A few minutes later, Daniel opened his hazel eyes. They were surrounded by singed eyelashes and topped by singed eyebrows. His attempt at speaking resulted in a coughing fit. I showed him the water bottle and told him to open his mouth and I poured a little in.

"Don't try to speak, Daniel. You inhaled too much smoke. Just rest." I lifted the water bottle to him again and said, "Here, have a bit more."

He tried to speak again, but this time he managed a few croaky words, "My father is dead."

# CHAPTER THIRTY-SEVEN

# Ava

"Oh God, Daniel. I'm so sorry. You were so lucky to get out."

I looked up at the redhead, "Thank you for saving him."

"Don't thank me yet. We still have to get off this roof and down the fire escape. I suggest we go."

With a critical eye she assessed Daniel, "Can you make it?"

He nodded and wheezed, " I won't be the problem." Indicating me with his gaze.

Red zeroed in on me. I didn't like that one bit. I narrowed my eyes back at her.

"You look fine to me. Let's go."

"Go ahead. We won't keep you," I said standing up on my shaky legs.

We were about the same height and met each other eye to eye. I kept my back straight and my head held high. I notched my chin up a bit higher—just for good measure.

"Look, the fire has diminished, but I wouldn't say we were out of danger. Let's go before the situation becomes critical," she told us both, though she continued to stare straight at me.

"Ava," Daniel interjected, "I can stay here with you. We can wait for the fire department to..."

Daniel wasn't able to finish his sentence as a coughing fit overtook him and he started audibly wheezing again.

"Your name is Ava?" The redhead asked, though for some reason she sounded surprised.

"Yes. And yours?"

"Scarlett, but I go by Scar."

"Okay, Scar. Daniel needs to get away from the smoke," I tried to say nonchalantly and failed.

"Ava, I'll be..." He was cut off again by his coughing.

Ignoring Daniel, I asked Scar, "Do you think he can make it down the stairs?"

"Well, there's only one way to find..."

Just then an explosion rocked the building and the club windows shattered in a shower of smoke, fire, and shards of glass.

"Fuck!" I yelled out, as I threw myself on top of Daniel—protecting him, since he was still coughing and was slow to move.

Scar looked down at me, completely unfazed by the explosion and said, "Can we go now?"

I think I could hate her and her unaffected demeanor. How could she be so calm when there had just been an explosion? Daniel and I helped each other to stand.

"Let's go," I said.

Scar was ahead of us and leading the way. Thankfully she didn't see me grab Daniel's hand, holding it in a death grip as we made our way towards the dreaded fire escape. I could feel the dread overtaking me. I knew I couldn't do this.

I didn't realize I was hyperventilating until we stopped just before the ledge and Scar turned to address me.

"What the fuck is the matter with you?" She asked, blue eyes narrowed.

"She...is...afraid...of heights..." Daniel supplied breathlessly, when I didn't answer.

"Get over yourself! Your friend here," she said pointing at Daniel for emphasis, "needs medical attention. And you are more than capable of getting down those stairs. He won't go unless you do. Do you want to kill him?"

I looked over at Daniel, he needed help. I could do this. I could totally do this.

"Fuck you! Come on, Daniel. Let's go."

Still gripping his hand, we marched over to the ledge —anger propelling me forward and gifting me with courage. Before that feeling could disappear, I stepped up onto the low wall and reached out to grip the arched railing. I didn't focus on the drop below me, but on getting Daniel to safety and to medical attention.

What if the smoke had damaged his ability to sing? I couldn't be the cause for further injury.

We had to get to safety. I could do this.

I heard the welcome sound of sirens fast approaching.

I turned on the top step and reached with pointed toes to the first rung of the ladder and stepped down. I wrapped my arms around the railing and hugged it tight for a moment.

A wave of nauseating pain overtook my stomach and bile splashed into the back of my throat. I had forgotten about the gouges in my arm until I was painfully reminded just then.

I hadn't made it very far when paralyzing fear crept through me.

My face was placed between the rungs of the ladder and I rested my forehead against the top step. I stared unblinking at the side of the old building, focusing on nothing but my breathing.

"Step down one more. I'm coming over." Scar said, as she stepped up and over the side, joining me on the ladder.

I had no choice but to move down or she would have stepped on me.

"Move another three steps so Daniel can come over too."

God, she was so bossy! I grumbled as I moved down another three steps.

We continued in this fashion, making it about halfway before Daniel needed to stop and catch his breath.

"Are you always so damned bossy?" I asked Scar.

She ignored my rhetorical question and asked one of her own instead.

"So tell me, Ava, what do you do for a living?"

We had stopped at a platform of sorts and waited for Daniel to say he was ready to continue. I was so shocked that I had made it halfway down, without falling to my death, that I answered without thinking about it.

"I was a principle dancer with the LA Ballet until my fiancé and I had to leave town unexpectedly. But I'm hoping to dance with another company soon, if not with the LA Ballet again."

"I'll be ready in just a minute. I'm breathing better away from the smoke," Daniel told us.

"That was a pretty rough club, what were you guys doing there?"

I looked at her through narrowed eyes and asked, "What were you doing there, Scar?"

"I needed to give the owner a message, but it had already been delivered by another messenger," she said, some unknown emotion lacing her words.

"Daniel and our friend, Willow, were contracted to play music for the club. I came to listen to their set. There was something off about that club, so we were leaving as soon as their set was over. But then the fire broke out.

Daniel looked at me with profound sadness in his eyes and said, "I lost my Martin. Damn it, I loved that guitar."

"Trey has it. He carried it down to safety. We would have never left it. We know how important it is to you."

"Thank you so much. We should be going."

The reprieve had been welcome, but now I would have to restart the whole process over again.

# CHAPTER THIRTY-EIGHT

# Sage

Traffic wasn't bad this time of night, thankfully. I shouldn't take too long to get to downtown. Thirty minutes, but maybe thirty minutes too late.

She'll be fine, Trey will go and get her. Knowing his personality, he'll forcibly carry her down if need be. I don't want that for her, but if it gets her off that burning building and down to safety—then so be it.

I reached out to Lieut. Clarke to see what was going on at Hotel Dark. He informed me that we had rescued sixty-three people. They were mostly women between the ages of fourteen and forty-seven, but there had been a handful of men as well.

They were in the process of going through the hotel currently, but didn't expect to find much there. They would search through each room, on each floor looking for any kind of evidence.

The prison cells at the hotel had all been outfitted the same. Just a bed and dirty linen, Clarke told me. I wondered what kind of condition the other sixty-two people were in.

Because Jade had been emaciated, I thought. And roughed up, with bruises littering her frail frame. Gripping the steering wheel tight, I wanted to go punch that fucktard in the face again and keep going until he lost consciousness.

We had to find a way to stop this madness.

These poor lost souls would now have to fight infection, forced drug addiction, and the demons that would rip at their minds. They would need psychological and emotional support. If they had a family to return to, they would all need counseling for the fallout. But for those who had left a bad home life—what would they have? Who would help them to cope and to transition back to a normal way of life?

Normal, a subjective concept—more like a new normal, because they could never go back to what was.

According to Clarke, they had found a cache of drugs located in what would be the office of the hotel. He said it appeared to be Rohypnol, ketamine, and possibly methamphetamine. But lab toxicologies on the victims, as well as an analysis of the drugs themselves, would confirm what they were and what they were given.

The Lieut. said there was very little food to be found and what was there had spoiled. That explained the methamphetamine—they were more than likely using it as an appetite suppressant.

The final update was to tell me about a room they had found on the bottom floor. It had been outfitted to allow members to participate in extreme BDSM. Clarke and his team onsite had found a large amount of blood in that room. Clarke and I agreed that the room was more than likely a way for sick assholes to torture people and use BDSM as an excuse and a cover. Because no true follower of the BDSM lifestyle would allow for that amount of bloodshed.

I was weary from the evil permeating this world we lived in. Weary from the death of innocents. But I would never give up—I fought for Ava, for Lilly, for Jade, and for all the nameless who had no one to stand for them.

Be safe, Ava. Be safe, I thought as I screeched to a stop down the street from the old building, as everything was blocked off by LAPD.

I saw smoke and fire funneling from the top of the building and into the night sky. Things did not look good.

LAFD had their ladder extended and were dousing the flames, but they were not making much progress.

I ran towards where I thought the fire escape would be located on the backside of the building.

When I saw Ava, I ran faster to reach her.

# CHAPTER THIRTY-NINE

# Ava

When we finally made it to the bottom, I was a jittery mess. LAFD had arrived, but we were out of danger, so they let us continue the descent on our own.

Daniel was taken away by paramedics to be assessed. He was still wheezing and coughing and needed to be given oxygen. I remained just outside the ambulance as they attended to him.

Trey and Willow joined me there.

Willow launched herself into my arms and was hugging me hard.

"I was so scared for you guys when I heard that explosion."

"I can't breathe, Willow."

Oh! Sorry," she said letting go quickly and stepping back next to Trey. "What happened up there?"

"A woman named Scar found Daniel and brought him out of the club. He was initially unconscious and having a hard time breathing. Once he was awake, the three of us were having a debate about climbing down the fire escape, when the club exploded and the windows shattered," I explained briefly.

"Holy shit!" Willow exclaimed.

"Needless to say, the negotiations for staying on the roof were blasted off the table. Besides, Daniel was having a difficult time breathing and that was the deciding factor."

"Why are you bleeding, Ava?" Trey asked, as he pointed to my arm.

I looked at my arm, having forgotten about the injury again. It amazed me what the mind could do for the body when otherwise occupied.

"Some drunken asshat pushed me when I didn't move out of her way. As graceful as usual, I stumbled and landed on the short wall that surrounds the rooftop. It's nothing, just a few scratches from some broken bricks."

"Looks to be more than just a few scratches," he said, disbelieving.

I shrugged, neither confirming nor denying.

"Does Sage know what's going on?" I asked Trey.

"I called him and he called you. You didn't talk to him?"

"No," I said, taking my cell phone out of my back pocket.

Several missed calls, voicemails, and text messages from Sage.

*I love you too*

*I'm on my way*

*Please stay safe*

I pressed the button for voice messages and put the phone to my ear.

"*Ava I'm on my way. Stay safe for me. I know you're terrified of heights, but I also know you can overcome those fears. You are the strongest of women. Look at what you've had to deal with this year—and you did it with such strength and grace—and only a few curse words."*

I laughed at his statement. I did cuss a lot.

*"I love you, Beauty. Thank you for loving me, despite my darkness. Now please, get off that roof and away from that burning building. You can do it! I know you can. Come down. Come home to me! I love you, Ava. With every breath, I love you."*

His message ended with his impassioned *I love you.* I wanted Sage here and now. I wanted to hold him. Show him that I did it. I made it off that damned roof and down the fire escape from *hell!*

I had been so afraid I'd fall over or throw myself over. It felt like it could have gone either way--not that I *would* throw myself over, it's just that weird sensation I get from being so afraid of heights.

"Thank you, Ava."

I heard, just before Sage pulled me into his arms and hugged the breath right out of me. But no worries on that front. I had no need for my own—as he gave me his breath to expand my lungs and his love to fill my heart. All my needs were met and I was home.

"I love you, Sage."

He pulled away to look me over. His hands and eyes caressing all of me. Assessing my health and searching for injuries. When he got to my arm, I flinched having forgotten about the stupid thing again.

"Let me see," he said, as he unwrapped the sash from my right upper arm. The material was sticking badly and he hadn't even made it to my skin yet.

"Trey, get some saline from the ambulance," Sage directed.

"It's nothing, truly. Please don't worry over it. Let's go see how Daniel is doing. We had to get him off that building and down here as fast as possible, his breathing didn't sound good."

I tried to redirect the attention away from me and towards Daniel. The scratches were burning like crazy and hurt like hell, especially now that they were the focus of all this attention.

"It's not going to work, Ava Grace DeLaney."

"Oh! You triple named me. I'm in trouble now," I giggled.

Sage looked up from my arm. I could see retribution and passion warring in his turbulent blue eyes.

"Yes, you are. But we can discuss that later—at home," he promised.

I shivered and flushed at the passionate promise contained within his bald statement.

Trey returned moments later and said, "The paramedics didn't want to give it up, not until I told them I was FBI. And still they gave me shit about pulling rank, because they want to look her over. 'It's what they get paid to do,' they told me succinctly."

Sage merely held his hand out for the saline and ignored the rest. He was too focused and attentive to the task at hand to address any of what Trey had said. He was too busy assessing the damage to my arm.

He poured the saline over the sash and slowly pried the material off of itself and then off of me. Once the gouges were exposed to the air, the pain increased exponentially. I sucked in a stuttering breath and held it while biting my lip and digging my nails into my palm to offset the pain in my arm.

"I'm sorry," he said when he heard my moan of pain. "How in the hell did you gouge your arm so bad?" he asked.

"I fell onto the wall surrounding the roof. The bricks are old and broken. They...they kind of ripped at my arm when I was falling over the edge," I confessed quietly, looking at the ground.

"Trey, please ask one of the paramedics to come here and make sure they bring their bag with them."

Sage reached with his right hand to tilt my chin up. I looked into his eyes, but I couldn't name the emotion that swam there.

"I'm so proud of you, Ava. That took a tremendous amount of courage."

"It wasn't courageous at all," I denied. "I was scared to death and shaking so bad, I had a hard time holding onto the railing as we came down the fire escape."

"That is the definition of courage, Ava. You put Daniel and his needs ahead of your own paralyzing fear of heights—bringing him to safety and to medical care."

"Stop shaking your head at me," he said, as he leaned forward to kiss my lips. "You're my hero."

I looked to my right as the paramedic approached us with his trauma bag in tow. I shook my head in disbelief and said, "Seriously, Brian? We have got to stop meeting like this. Are there no other paramedics in all of LA?" I laughed.

"Well now, Ava, apparently I am the only one that matters," he said laughing too, but then sobered and said, "Let me have a look at that arm."

"It's nothing, really," I said as I lifted my arm for him to assess.

"Let me be the judge of that," he said as he looked over the bloody gouges. "I'm afraid you might need stitches. At the very least, it needs to be cleaned out. When was your last tetanus shot?"

"I'm good up to date. Do I have to go to the hospital? Or can you clean it here?"

I had no desire to go to the hospital again. I'd spent way too much time there.

"I can clean and bandage your arm, but you need to have it evaluated," he said more to Sage than to me.

I huffed at the two them. I knew they just wanted what was best for me, but I was standing right there after all.

"I'll be sure that she makes it to the doctor, that's a promise. But could you fix her up, at least temporarily?" Sage asked, as he looked at his watch.

As Brian gathered his supplies, I sat on a car bumper and looked around. Sage was on his phone reading text messages. Trey was talking to LAPD about what he knew about the club fire. I was hoping he would fill them in so well that I wouldn't have to chat too.

Brain came over and used an antibacterial wash to gently cleanse my arm.

"Good Lord, that hurts like a bitch!" I exclaimed when he began cleaning my arm. "Is that battery acid?" I asked and laughed, though it wasn't really funny.

It was either laugh or start bawling like a two year old.

"Almost finished. I'll just rinse you off and wrap a bandage around it," he said and then finished quicker than I had expected.

"Thank you, Brian, for attending to me again."

"Think nothing of it. Try to stay safe and injury free from now on," he said as he returned to the ambulance.

When my attention came back to Sage he was looking decidedly unnerved. He was looking off into space, not really focused on the here and now, or so it seemed to me.

He read the text messages on his phone again and searched the crowd looking for something or someone. He stepped in front of me, almost protectively.

I peeked around Sage and searched the crowd in the general direction of where he was looking—searching for the odd man out. There were clubbers from Nitro, LAPD, and LAFD everywhere.

I saw that redhead, Scar, on her phone. I saw my savior guy, who looked over when he saw me looking in his direction. I nodded my head in delayed gratitude and thanks. Nothing out of the ordinary stood out.

Sage sucked in a shocked breath and exhaled a quiet,"Un-fucking-believeable."

# CHAPTER FORTY

# Sage

Multiple texts were buzzing my wrist in rapid succession. Initially, I ignored the incessant vibrations, too busy with trying to get medical attention for Ava. But then I worried that Lieut. Clarke was reaching out to me about Hotel Dark.

Ava kept claiming her 'scratches' were nothing, but that wasn't the case. They were deep gouges marring the soft, sensitive skin on the inside of her upper arm. I couldn't imagine how much they must hurt. They were a bloody mess.

Paramedic Brian happened to be on duty tonight and was attending to Ava. So when the buzzing continued I grabbed my phone to see what was going on.

An unknown number had sent the same text repeatedly.

*Look.*

I looked up and around—searching, clueless as to who this was and what they wanted. Could it somehow be Ivan? I stepped over and in front of Ava, though she was still mostly unprotected if he were to have a gun.

LAPD, LAFD, and crowds of people were roaming about the streets in front of me. A controlled chaos that the beat officers were handling with calm professionalism. I searched every face, my eyes restless, looking for the threat I felt in my bones.

My gaze touched briefly upon a redhead that happened to be looking in my direction. With a single glance, I took her all in, categorizing and memorizing her details.

Red hair piled on top of her head, tallish, a messenger bag slung over her shoulder, jeans, and a black jacket. I moved on and continued searching the crowds when she dropped her attention back to her phone.

The buzzing, buzzing, buzzing of my wrist and phone.

*You look, but you don't see.*

*Look, Sage.*

*Look and see me.*

Searching again, but with no idea who I was seeking. I looked to the right and then the left. I saw the redhead—staring straight at me again. She did seem familiar, but I didn't know any redheads, except Willow.

This time, I really looked at her, searching her face and eyes—though she was quite a distance away. The poor lighting didn't help me to assess her features.

Buzzing again.

*I can't have changed that much.*

*Think blonde hair.*

This game was getting old, I thought, but played along and envisioned her with blonde hair. And it all clicked into place. She knew the second I figured it out who she was because gave a little wave, then was texting again.

Buzzing.

*Took you long enough.*

My attention bounced back and forth between staring at her in disbelief and to reading the messages she fired at me.

*It's been a long time, lover.*

*So long—you didn't even recognize me.*

Where have you been? I texted.

*Away.*

Why are you here.

*To kill Ivan, among other things.*

*You saw the folder.*

Yes—how did you know?

*Notification tracker.*

I see.

*Congratulations, by the way.*

*Your fiancée is beautiful...*

I turned to look at Ava and thought to myself, how could she have known that we were engaged?

*But she's more than that.*

*She's courageous and fearless.*

She is that and so much more.

*She was terrified on that roof.*

Of heights, yes.

*But she rose above.*

She's my hero—my light.

*I can see why.*

What do you want, Tomi?

*To say goodbye, Sage.*

*And to thank you.*

For what?

*Trying to avenge my Emma.*

*It was Ivan all along.*

*He's evil and he's dead.*
*So you can let it go.*
He's dead? Are you sure?
*Yes, but you need to step away.*
I don't think I can.
It's bigger than Ivan.
*You will.*
Oh, will I?
*Yes, to protect Ava.*
*Think of her.*
*You can't save me.*
*And you can't avenge Emma.*
*We are both beyond help.*
Tomi?
*No Sage.*
*Consider me gone and Tomi dead.*
*I won't be coming back.*
*I've a mission elsewhere.*
Where you going?
*You don't need to know.*
Tomi, stop playing games.
*I'm not the same and like I said, Tomi is dead.*
Talk to me.
Tell me what you need.
How can I help?
*Always the Savior.*
*Never change, Sage.*

# CHAPTER FORTY-ONE

# Sage

"Un-fucking-believeable."

"Sage, what's the matter?"

"I just read some unbelievable texts. And if I didn't know better, I would think it was some kind of a hoax. But it's not and that makes it all the more disturbing."

"Good Lord! Why'd she do that?" Ava asked, incredulous.

"I turned to her and asked, "What?""

"Scar. She just destroyed her phone."

"Who's Scar?" I asked confused.

"Scarlett, the redhead across the way from us," she said pointing to where Tomi had been standing.

"Is that what she said her name was?"

"Yes. When she brought Daniel out of the club, she said her name was Scarlett, but to call her Scar."

"Did she?" I asked.

"We can ask her, she's right there."

When we turned back to where Scar had been standing, she was already gone.

"Kind of a bully that one." Ava huffed, "The whole way down the fire escape, she kept telling me what to do."

"Ava," I said, "her name isn't Scar."

"No? How would you know that? Do you know her somehow?"

"I did at one time, but not anymore."

"That doesn't make any sense."

"You know her too—but as Tomi Delacourt."

"But...but I thought she was dead."

"We thought she was. I don't know what's going on with her. Only that she texted to tell me that Ivan was dead."

"Ivan is dead? Truly, Sage?" She asked hopefully.

"Tomi returned to LA for vengeance. She wanted to kill Ivan, but somebody beat her to the trigger."

"She doesn't look anything like what I had imagined," Ava said.

"I didn't recognize her at all, and she was practically standing in front of me."

"Why'd she destroy her phone? That's weird."

I knew exactly why she destroyed her phone—so we couldn't track her. Bur before answering Ava, I searched the crowd one more time for Scar. I found her a ways down the street about to disappear around the building.

She stopped, looked back over her shoulder and gave a small salute goodbye—before disappearing forever.

I pulled Ava into my arms and held her tight, though mindful of her arm. I silently thanked Scar—she knew exactly what she had been doing when she bullied Ava down that fire escape. I also thanked whoever had killed Ivan because now Ava would be safe from his sadistic machinations.

# CHAPTER FORTY-TWO

# Ava

**Six Months Later**

I have been staying at my father's house in the Palisades for over six months now. I was sitting outside on the terrace enjoying a cup of coffee and the late morning sun. The lingering fog from the coast had just began to lift, and it was turning out to be the perfect spring day.

I hadn't seen Sage for a couple of weeks now. But would finally see him later today. He'd been occupied with the LAPD and the FBI. They were still sorting through what details they could find surrounding Ivan Dubrovsky's death, the human trafficking case, the club fire, the death of Creighton, as well as Tomi's disappearance five years ago, her reappearance, and now her subsequent disappearance.

I was still trying to wrap my head around the fact that Scar, the woman who had rescued Daniel from the club fire, was none other than Tomi Delacourt: former Deputy District Attorney and Sage's ex-lover.

Sage had told me that five years ago when she had disappeared, she had gone off the grid to discover who had actually killed her family. Her mission had been to discover their identity and to seek vengeance.

Of course she'd gone missing yet again and Sage was worried over her mental and emotional stability. She had been hyper-focused on vengeance and retribution, yet she had been denied what she thought was her duty and her right—to kill Ivan.

*Eye for an eye*, his life for her daughter, Emma's. But some unknown person had killed him before she'd had the chance.

I can't imagine how hard that would be. She probably spent the past five years of her life preparing for her vengeance, only to have it snatched out of her hands at the very last moment.

Not that I agree with vigilante justice, but I understood given that he had killed her daughter. I wouldn't sit in judgment of her motivations. Because if somebody were to kill Sage or one of my family members, who's to say how I would respond.

"Good morning, darling," Alexei said when he walked onto the terrace and kissed my forehead.

"Good morning."

"Sage just phoned and said he'd be here in a couple hours."

"Perfect. Willow and Riley will be here in a few minutes for a late lunch." I took a sip of my coffee, then said, "Thank you for opening your home for today."

"Ava, I love you. I would do anything for you. Give you anything that you needed. There's no recompense that I can offer you for the years that were stolen from us. But I can give you my now and my future." He paused a moment before continuing, "We both suffered due to the machinations of that sadistic man. I would have never guessed at the true depth of his evil. I don't think anyone could have."

"No, it's unbelievable how one man could destroy so many lives. But we've had to live with the consequences of his diabolical actions. They changed the course and the very fabric of our lives. I would have loved to live the life that we were meant to live—as a family."

I couldn't keep the emotion from my voice or from showing on my face. But then neither could Alexei. He stepped towards me and I stood so that we could embrace in grief and in love.

"Grace and Chloe will always be with you, Ava. He can't take that from you."

"I know. Some days I feel them like a gentle caress. While other days, their love surrounds me like a strong, warm embrace."

"Good. Now, do you need help with anything before the girls arrive?"

"No, everything is ready. I'm just waiting them to get here," I said, sitting back down.

"I'll leave you to enjoy a little peace and solitude before Willow gets here. Because we both know that it won't be Riley talking nonstop," he said and we both laughed.

I loved my flamboyant Willow and my reserved Riley. They were the best friends a girl could have and they were truly the soul sisters of my heart.

Willow and I could not have been more excited when Riley told us that she was moving to California to make LA her home.

She wasn't living here yet. This was just a quick visit on her part. She had to sign closing documents on her Hollywood bungalow, but she was here long enough that we were able to spend some time together.

We were expecting Mason and Daniel to stop by a little later as well. Mason had hurt his shoulder last season and was on the injured reserve list. He was seeing a shoulder specialist at UCLA, so Mason and Daniel would be here too.

I couldn't wait to see everyone and to get caught up on everyone lives.

"Ava?"

"Yes?" I said, not turning around.

"There's someone here to see you."

I stood and turned at the strange tone in my father's voice. I was completely shocked by who was standing behind him.

# CHAPTER FORTY-THREE

# Sage

Over the past six months, Trey, Lieut. Clarke, and I had continued to investigate the Dark folder that Brent had compiled. We followed up on every lead and dead end—even though the trail originating from that folder had grown beyond cold at this point.

The information that we were collecting about this secret group had created a bleak picture that was dark, but abstract—at best. We knew The Dark were involved heavily in human trafficking through domestic and international black markets. But that was only a fraction of what their criminal activities entailed.

They were housed primarily in Europe. So in light of the geographical scope of this investigation, the FBI was taking over jurisdiction and in my opinion—good riddance. The whole business had been an exercise in frustration that took me away from my Ava. Plus, I had no desire or aspirations to be the lead investigator on a case that would include traveling all over the US and Europe. But if I had wanted to continue on as that lead investigator, I could have.

"Sage, the FBI would like to bring you on board. We'd love for you to continue as lead investigator here in the US. We wouldn't need you for the international angle, as we already have someone on that," Trey had informed me a few weeks ago during our weekly meeting.

"I would say that I was surprised, but I'm not. You haven't exactly been subtle about dropping hints," I replied.

"You know you're great at undercover work and we need someone who's already up to speed. This case will explode eventually and it could catapult your career to the next level."

"I can't deny that I'm intrigued by the possibilities and the potential. Of course I had always thought to eventually make a bid for the FBI."

"Perfect, we would make a great team, Sage. I'd be your point of contact, just like what you've had with the Lieut. And..."

"But, I'm not interested," I told Trey, cutting him off. No deliberation was needed. "Life changes and we change with it." I finished.

Ava was my game changer.

Trey and I had been tying up loose ends this past month—striving for a seamless transfer between Trey and I and the new FBI team assigned to the case. This new team would be investigating the Dark folder, Ivan, and the secret society.

This case had been all evil and darkness—and I felt saturated in the remnants. It would never leave me, but as of yesterday, I was no longer involved with the active investigation. I was thankful to be done with it. I had other, more important things to focus on.

One bright spot was that Officer Peacock had been arrested the same night as the raid on Hotel Dark. The LAPD had found incriminating evidence on his computer that he had yet to destroy when the warrant was served. He was still in jail awaiting trial, as he was considered a flight risk.

Jade, the girl we had found at Hotel Dark, had been reunited with her family. She was a witness for the state and was attempting to identify club members that had frequented the hotel. That was proving to be very difficult, as she had been drugged for portions of her time at Hotel Dark.

Dr. Wong kept us informed as to her medical condition and her overall progress. She was recovering physically and remained in counseling for the emotional and psychological support. She was attending a support group here in LA.

Jade had decided to stay in LA and continue to pursue her dreams of becoming an actress. During one of our many interviews, she had told me that she was determined to succeed. She decided that she wouldn't let those assholes from Hotel Dark dictate her entire life. She wouldn't let those dark days define who she was and who she would be.

What a warrior. She was strong, just like my Ava. And given enough time, I thought Jade would find her way through this darkness that she was currently drowning in.

I understood her determination, though only from the perspective of watching Ava and other victims navigate their way through the aftermath and fallout from their abductions.No one came away unscathed, far from it.

I still had a few errands left to run before I could drive over to Alexei's to see Ava. We chatted regularly on the phone and texted every day, but we had been separated for weeks now. I refused to allow another day to pass without seeing her again, without holding her in my arms, without loving her breathless.

God I missed her with an unfathomable ache.

# CHAPTER FORTY-FOUR

# Ava

Standing behind my father was Daniel's mother, Dolores Creighton. She was a long way from home. I couldn't imagine what she could possibly want though I wondered if she somehow knew that Mason and Daniel were visiting today.

Surely not. How could she?

"Dotty, so nice to see you." I greeted her affectionately with a hug and a kiss to her cheek.

"I'll leave you two to visit. Ava let me know if you need anything." Alexei turned to Dotty and said, "It was nice to meet you, Dolores. Perhaps we can chat again later," before turning to leave us alone.

"Dotty, you're a long way from Palm Springs. Let me get you something to drink. Are you hungry?"

I had always loved her, though I hadn't understood her relationship with her husband, Quinton. But, as an adult and reflecting back, I understood it now—or I thought that I did.

Their relationship was toxic. Daniel's father had been an extremely domineering man; he had been psychologically and physically abusive to his wife and eldest son—for years.

In retrospect, I could see the signs now that I didn't as a child. And it wasn't a pretty picture that my mind created. I wish I would have known, not that I could have made a difference back then. But I could now.

"Please, don't go to any trouble," she said.

"It's no trouble at all. Please, sit," I said, pouring her a sparkling water. "You're looking well. How was your trip away? It's been over six months now," I continued, when I joined her at the table.

"Thank you. Initially it was difficult. I had to adjust to a new way of life and a new way of thinking," she paused, as if inwardly reflecting, "but, the time away was just what I needed. Time to heal and time to reflect on the past and prepare for the future."

"I'm so happy to hear that," I said, genuinely relieved that she seemed to be coping.

It had been over six months since her husband, Quinton, had died. And I had never seen her look more beautiful than she did in this moment. She had cut her sandy blonde hair into a Twiggy-like hairstyle—short and sleek. She and Daniel shared the same expressive hazel eyes. She was thin, but now she looked fit instead of stressed.

Daniel had told me that the last time he had seen his mother was at his father's funeral. Dotty had taken off right after to go on a sabbatical of sorts—telling Daniel that she needed to get her head screwed on straight.

"Do you know what today is, Dotty?"

"Yes, I do and I don't wish to impose. I've only just arrived back in town and was hoping to speak with Daniel. I would be happy to come back later."

"There's no need to come back later. Mason and Daniel should be here in just a little while. I know that Daniel would love to see you. He's been worried, you know."

"I didn't want him to worry," she said looking away, "but, I couldn't stay in Palm Springs anymore and just needed to get away."

"He knows, Dotty, and understands."

"My doctors recommended that I leave for a while. They also recommended that I not make any rash decisions during the first six months. So I left to be sure that I didn't."

"I understand."

And I really did. I had also waited for over six months to make any life changes. Especially since Sage and I were still dealing with the fallout from six months ago—when we had returned to LA for Sage to investigate Tomi's death.

For the most part, the FBI had jurisdiction over the investigation now. So Sage was helping as a consultant, but not as an active participant. He said the investigation was leading in a direction that was far beyond his scope and that of the LAPD.

Sage told me that Trey was still involved, but that Trey, as a lead investigator, had a very large caseload of ongoing investigations. Sage hadn't seen him in a while, but Willow had.

"My girlfriends, Willow and Riley, will be here soon. We are having lunch; why don't you join us? You'll love them," I invited.

She looked shell-shocked, taken off guard by the invitation. "Oh, I couldn't."

"Oh, but you could!"

She smiled, "Thank you, Ava. I would love to join you girls."

"Just be warned, Willow is crazy and nonstop and Riley is quiet and reserved. They are both such incredible musicians. Willow plays the violin and Riley the piano."

"I know," she said quietly. "I saw them perform with you last year. You have always been such an exquisite dancer, even as a child. While Chloe was a magnificent teacher and ballerina, she saw true talent in you and did everything she could to foster its growth. She loved you endlessly."

"And I loved her. She was my rock. I miss her so much," I said, my voice subdued with emotion.

"She was my best friend; I bet you don't remember that."

"No, I didn't. I'm sorry."

"She was a smart lady and uniquely eccentric. She hated Quinton with a passion. Chloe told me to leave him, on more than one occasion, over bottles of wine. I didn't listen, though I should have. I just couldn't envision how I would survive by leaving the only life that I knew. By staying, I did my boys a disservice. Quinton was not a good father and role model. Hopefully I can make amends to them."

"Daniel loves you. He'll listen, just talk to him."

"I plan to. He needs to know the truth about a lot of things—including who really bought his Martin guitar for him."

I looked at her in surprise, and she nodded her head in acknowledgment. We assumed that Mason had bought it for Daniel. But clearly Mason had known the truth and he had kept her secret for all of these years.

I reached out my hand, grabbing hers in support. She graced me with a beautiful, thankful smile.

"Who's ready to get the party started?" Willow's infectious voice queried from the terrace doors.

I rolled my eyes at Dotty and said with a huge smile, "You see what I have to put up with?"

Turning to greet Willow, I saw that Riley was there as well and quiet as usual though she was smiling just as brightly as the rest of us.

"Well, come over here and give me a hug you two. I haven't seen you guys in forever."

I opened my arms and we had one big fat hug-fest. We were giggling and hugging and carrying on like a bunch of loons. When we finally broke apart, with much laughter and just a few tears, I introduced Dotty.

They both welcomed her, making her feel as part of our group and not as an interloper. As we sat down to lunch, I had an epiphany. Today was a special day—on so many levels and I wanted to include Dotty in on this. She deserved a bit of happiness.

I hoped she could see that too and would agree.

# CHAPTER FORTY-FIVE

# Ava

"Oh no, I couldn't, " Dotty protested.

"But you will, because I asked so sweetly and today is *my* day. So, I should get whatever I want."

I was laughing so hard at the look on her face when I said that. I sounded self-centered and spoiled, but I wasn't. Well, maybe just a little. But I think I deserved it, if just a little—and at least for today.

"Okay, I'll do it," she said reluctantly, but with a huge smile brightening her face.

"I never thought to have an opportunity like this. Ever. Thank you, Ava."

"You're doing me a favor, I told you that. But you're welcome."

I looked around the bedroom where I had been staying these past six months. It was a beautiful room and I would miss it. But I was more than ready to go home.

Everything seemed to be safe now and according to the FBI, I was no longer in danger. So I was free to return to my life. Though I actually already had. I was performing with a dance company that fit me more than the LA Ballet ever could. I was making great friends there, though admittedly I was still weary, given what had happened with Marcus and Ivan.

They were both dead now and no longer deserved my time or attention. I would no longer think of them or the pain they had caused me. They would be relegated to the past and I would bury them under a mountain of happiness that their toxic waste could never breach.

"Are you ready, Ava?" Willow asked, pulling back to the here and now.

"Almost," I said, as I grabbed a few more things before we left the room to go downstairs.

There was a knock at the door and I heard my father's voice call my name.

"Ava, are you ready? Sage is here."

I walked over and opened the door. The look on his face was priceless and one I would forever remember.

"You..." he stopped to swallow the tears that had gathered in his silver eyes, "You look so beautiful, Ava. So much like Grace."

"Thank you," I said simply, but with equal emotion.

"Sage asked me to give you this," he said handing me an envelope.

"Ladies, let's wait outside for a moment. Then it'll be time to go."

Each one of them came to give me a kiss and then headed out the door. I watched them leave, Dotty escorted out by my father, his hand low on her back in support.

I wonder if? My mind swirled with the possibilities on that front.

I opened the envelope and read the note within.

I fought back the tears that threatened to choke me, and I wondered how he could do this to me—today of all days.

I gathered my courage and my love, then walked serenely down the stairs where everyone was waiting for me. I missed Sage and couldn't wait to see him, even though he made me cry.

We'd have a chat about that later.

I loved how my long chestnut hair swayed back and forth, tickling my arms as I walked. It reached past my butt, I should trim it, but I wouldn't. I typically wore it up and in a bun. I hated having to fuss with it. But Sage loved my hair; loved it long and loose. So today I wore it long and styled just for him.

My father reached for my hand as I made it to the bottom of the stairs.

"You have a beautiful soul and a generous heart to include Dolores. Knowing her situation, this may be just what she needed to finish healing her wounded spirit."

"Yes, I thought so too. She's a lovely woman, Alexei. I have always adored her. She was best friends with Chloe, though I didn't realize that."

"Yes, she is very lovely," he said, as he looked over to her.

I saw her blush under his scrutiny. Well, what do we have here. I looked up to him and he was simply enamored. Healing for both of them perhaps.

"Are you ready, darling?" Alexei asked.

"Please, I want to see Sage."

"Then let's proceed. Places everyone," Alexei instructed.

# CHAPTER FORTY-SIX

# Ava

We headed towards the gardens at the side of the house, where Sage and everyone else were waiting. It was a beautiful day, the third of June to be exact. I had been looking forward to this event for months now, and I couldn't have chosen a more perfect day.

I loved all things retro and today was no different. I wore a LouLou 50s tea length strapless dress in ivory satin with a silk organza jacket, cinched with a wide satin belt and silk covered buckle. It was very elegant and feminine and I loved everything about it.

A gentle breeze coming from the coast caught the skirt of my dress causing it to flirt and dance around my calves as we made our way to the gardens.

Alexei stopped just before the entrance and turned me to look at him.

"Ava, I don't even know where to begin," he said holding my hands. "A year ago, I couldn't have imagined this reality. Not for one second."

"I know, I feel the same way. Life has taken me on a very unpredictable journey, but that circuitous road led me to you and to Sage. So in that regard, I couldn't be happier."

"You were taken from me at such a young age. I never thought to have you in my life again. But now that you're here and we've reunited, I don't want to lose you again."

"You won't, Alexei. I'm not going anywhere. You're stuck with me, Sage, and my crazy friends."

"I am so proud to be your father, Ava. I love you."

"I'm so thankful that we found each other after all these years. I love you, father."

We stood awhile, absorbing the moment and allowing our emotions to settle. We turned together and walked to the garden entrance—every step taking me home.

Willow began playing Johann Pachelbel, Canon in D Major when she saw us.

And suddenly my heart was racing.

Riley stood on the left as a bridesmaid. Willow would take her place, as my maid of honor, once she had finished playing her violin. Trey and Daniel were on my right—standing up with Sage.

Mason was next to Dotty in the front row. She loved them so much and would be very supportive of their relationship. I just knew it. The problem had always been Daniel's father, not her.

The small gathering stood when the music started and turned. All eyes were on Alexei, as father of the bride—and on me, the bride.

But I only had eyes for Sage, and they were starving for the sight of him. It had been weeks since I had visually feasted upon him.

My heart leapt into my throat. I wanted to run down the aisle to throw myself into his arms. I wanted to, but

I wouldn't. Nope, I would channel my inner Kate Middleton and my new twin mottos—poise and elegance—not tripping and falling.

Today was my wedding day, and everything would be perfect. But to ward off evil spirits hellbent on ruining my perfection, I crossed my fingers for added protection and nearly fumbled my flowers in the process.

"Are you ready, Ava?" Alexei inquired, when it sounded like I was hyperventilating.

"I am very ready. Just attempting to calm my racing heart and trembling hands," I said and showed him how my flowers were about to shake their petals right off.

"Close your eyes."

I did as Alexei instructed.

"Now, take a deep breath and think about how much Sage loves you. Then open your eyes and focus only on him."

When I reopened my eyes, I looked directly at Sage. And I was hit by the clarity and the intensity of his bright blue eyes. Unable to look away, I was held captive within forever.

Just like that first night when I had quite literally fallen into Sage's arms.

That night, Sage had ushered me gently towards that point of darkness, that oblivion I had craved, and finally my world of pain had been chased away. Technically, I had passed out in his arms and had scared the hell out of him. Or so he had later told me.

I had been completely vulnerable in that moment, but he'd stayed with me until the ambulance had arrived—cradling my abused body in his strong arms. They'd brought me to the hospital for treatment and he had remained by my side, acting as a surrogate for my absent family.

Tonight, he brought me home with the devotion and promise apparent in his magnetic gaze.

Alexei and I started down the aisle, slow and steady, keeping time with Willow's violin. Alexei had a firm hold of my arm so that I wouldn't trip and fall in my haste to get to Sage as fast as I could. I made it the first few feet without issue. No crying or tripping—a win, I'd say.

Keeping my gaze fixed firmly on Sage, I caressed his beautiful face with my eyes, so I saw the exact moment he set free his prized control. And I wanted to dive into the pool of emotions swimming in his blue depths—where I knew I'd float buoyant on the current of his love.

My thoughts were poetic and my heart was overflowing with emotion. I just knew my vows were going to be a jumbled mess, but luckily Sage understood Ava-babble.

But then I completely lost it. God I was afraid I would start ugly crying, but I couldn't care less.

My man allowed his tears to fall unashamedly. They rolled down his strong jaw and he wore those shiny trails with pride—declining to wipe away their evidence.

Tears of love were flowing freely by the time I stood before Sage. Alexei handed me over and into his care.

"Please stop crying, Beauty."

"I'll stop, if you stop," I replied with a smile.

I reached up to brush my fingers along the clear evidence of his emotion and love. The tips came away wet with his tears and I brushed them across my lips, not caring about the people gathered behind us or the minister before us.

Sage leaned down to kiss my anointed lips and we began—and continued—as husband and wife.

# CHAPTER FORTY-SEVEN

# Ava

After the ceremony and reception, Sage and I took off for our honeymoon. We had both decided to stay in the US instead of traveling abroad, like a fair number of newlyweds do. We didn't feel like hassling with flying somewhere.

We drove the Mustang up the coast to Santa Barbara and stayed at the San Ysidro Ranch. We had booked the Gardenia Cottage for a week. It was dark when we arrived and checked in, so the staff showed us to our cottage. It was exquisite and I couldn't wait to explore it tomorrow in the light of day.

We freshened up and then sat on the old fashioned porch, sipping champagne and relaxing.

"I love you, Ava," Sage told me, while holding my hand and caressing my wedding ring.

He raised his glass and said, "Here's to a lifetime of love and happiness. Thank you for loving me through the darkness, Beauty," he finished, clinking his glass to mine.

We both sipped at our champagne and finished the bottle while we chatted about how incredible the day had turned out to be. I explained to him how when Dotty had shown up, I asked to her to stay and to stand up for Grace and Chloe, as mother of the bride.

"She cried when I asked her, bless her heart. She's had it rough her entire adult life because of Daniel's father. She'll be a huge supporter of Mason and Daniel's relationship. Did you see the three of them chatting at the reception?"

"I did. She's a beautiful woman. I noticed that Alexei seemed to think so too," he said with a wink.

"Do you think? That Alexei was interested in Dotty? That would be great. I hate that he has been alone for all of these years."

"They have to find their own way, like Mason and Daniel, but I wouldn't be surprised at all if they chose to date."

It was getting late and I was getting sleepy.

"No falling asleep," Sage said teasing, "I still need to have my wicked way with my wife!"

"Ha, your wife is just relaxed, that's all. Not sleepy in the least," I said with a yawn and a smile.

"I have a gift for you, Ava. Let me go grab it," he told me, as he went back into the cottage.

When Sage returned, he handed me a small box that had been tied with a blue bow.

"Open it. It's my wedding present to you," he said hesitantly.

After untying the bow, I opened the box by lifting the lid. I stared at my gift, uncomprehending.

I looked at Sage and said, "I don't understand."

"First, I should probably tell you that financially we are fine. Better than fine. Grandpa Pete left me everything. I don't have to work, if I don't want to."

"Okay, though I wasn't worried about that. You have a job, and I have a job with the dance company. I don't think we'll starve or be homeless any time soon."

"No, we won't. But about that..." he said hedging. "As of today, I'm technically unemployed. I retired from the force."

I looked up at him and watched as he paced back and forth, hands shoved into his pockets. I lifted his detective's badge out of the box, where it had been nestled in a bed of blue velvet. I ran my finger over the cool metal and thought how this was the symbolic shield for my warrior.

The motto, 'to protect and to serve' was the summation of who and what Sage was, as a person and as a detective. There was no way he could leave that behind; it was integral to his identity.

"You gave up your job? For me?" I asked astounded.

"I would do anything for you, Ava, absolutely anything."

"But why would you quit your job?"

"I retired for multiple reasons. But if I had to choose one reason, it would be to protect you from the evil that I had to associate with in order to investigate these amoral, conscienceless criminals. If their darkness was already contaminating me, then by way of association, it would contaminate you."

I put the box with his badge on the table next to me and stood, walking to him and into his arms.

"I know that the darkness and the evil will always be there. But that doesn't mean I need to have a conversation with them every day," Sage said, pulling me in close.

"I love you, Sage. Thank you for my wedding present. If you want to step away and retire from the force, then I will support you in that decision. But, I don't need you to do that for me. I can handle your darkness. The innocent victims out there need people like you. They need people who can make a difference. They need you on their side and fighting for them," I said looking up at him.

"I'm relieved you feel that way because I'm not stepping away entirely. Over the past six months, while finishing the Ivan case, I decided that the LAPD was no longer where I wanted to be. I contemplated working for FBI, and Trey offered me a job, but I turned them down."

"I'm not sad about that, I have to admit," I told Sage, but then added, "And I might junk punch Trey the next time that I see him—just for trying to take you away from me."

Sage barked out a laugh and said, "I love your blood thirsty side. My odds are on you," he said, kissing me hard and fast.

"My idea is to approach it from a different angle, so I formed a private security company. I've hired a few other detectives and officers—all retired or retiring, but still wanting to continue the fight, but on their terms."

"What a great idea!" I said, and could see the relief on his face and in his smile. God, that dimple!

"It's still fluid and in its infancy, but I have an idea, a rough plan, and people interested in coming along to fight the good fight."

"I'll be right by your side, helping in any way that I can, Sage."

"I know that you will."

He leaned down and caressed my mouth with his. His lips brushing against mine, begging for permission. I opened my mouth and he dove right in to kiss me with all the love, devotion, and passion overflowing from his heart. My head spun, intoxicated by him and the champagne.

Sage pulled back, but with his lips still brushing softly against mine and said, "With my every breath, I will love you. With everything that I am, I will love you. You own me, Ava, every part of me is yours."

I pulled away and cradled the sides of his face with my hands. I looked at Sage and gave him the vow I was too nervous to give him at our wedding. My heart spoke to his—unencumbered and just free to be.

"I will love you through darkness and light, through pain and joy and through every day that I am blessed with life, Sage. You are mine, and I am forever yours."

THE END

# ABOUT PARIS ANDREN

Paris Andren is an emerging author who likes to write in multiple genres including: Romantic Suspense, Thriller, and Crime Fiction—all three contained within this first series—and she has an Urban Fantasy novel and Medical Series coming in 2017.

If you enjoyed *Web of Darkness* and would like to leave a review, it would be greatly appreciated. Social proof and reader input are incredibly valuable.

Thank you in advance for your time.

Sign up for Paris Andren's No Spam Newsletter for advanced reader access, notice for discounts on new releases, and a chance for free swag.
http://www.pariswrites.com/paris-press-release/